Copyright © 2024 Tilt-A-Whirl Publishing LLC

All rights reserved.

No part of this book may be reproduced in any form or by any electronic or mechanical means, including information storage and retrieval systems, without written permission from the author, except for the use of brief quotations in a book review.

This book is a work of a fiction. Any references to historical events, real people, or real places are used fictitiously. Any resemblance to actual events or people, living or dead, is purely coincidental.

Version 04012024

Cover Image: Deposit Photos

Formatting/Inner Images/Wrap: Dragonfly Graphic Designs

Editor: M.A. Patrick

Copy/Line Edit: Jasmine Arena

# Catch My EYE

## ARIANA ST. CLAIRE

### OVERTIME

*For the girls who wish for the one who will make all our fantasies come true...*

*And the ones who grant us our wishes...*

*Always and Forever.*

# PROLOGUE

## TY

*D*arkness cloaked me, a disguise I didn't wear lightly. The dark hid secrets, but it also became a safe place, without judgment or fear, on the nights when the world became too much. When the intricate details and false narratives brought about the damnation of people who didn't bother to look beyond themselves.

Maybe it was foolish to stand out here, lurking in the shadows. Watching her. Tracking her movements. Her head tilted to the side as she sat on her couch, feet curled up underneath her. Her favorite blanket tucked around her body, holding and keeping her safe within its embrace. Fingers flying over the letters on the keyboard, forming words and thoughts of people who didn't exist anywhere except her head or on the page as the stories spilled from her mind.

My eyes watched as her lips softly parted, brows occasionally drawn together when she stumbled upon a place that caused her to pause until she figured out how to keep going.

Enraptured by every infinitesimal movement. Every

slight nuance of emotion that played upon her face. Eyes lighting up, lips pouting or sometimes pursed in consternation. Pink tongue darting out, leaving a trace of wetness that had my cock straining in protest.

Fuck, it was sexy. Mesmerizing, even. The slender nape of her neck tempted. Called to me, begging to be touched. Held. Encircled. My hands twitched at my side, flexing as I drew in a breath. Eyes never leaving her. Dark tendrils snuck out of the high ponytail she gathered her hair up into earlier as she paused, caressing her skin the way I longed to. Fingers toying with the ends as she chewed at her bottom lip.

But when her gray eyes lit up? That was the moment I waited for, the second I couldn't look away from. Not that she'd ever know I was there.

Or how I knew the tiniest details about her. How she liked her coffee. Which side of the couch she favored. The walk she took only on rainy days, joy written all over her face, black umbrella with a Mary Poppins handle in her grip.

Every Friday. Red lingerie.

Wednesdays, she took a bubble bath with a glass of white wine. Three ice cubes.

Three tacos, two salsas, and Pom Guac with a dragon fruit margarita extra lime at the Prickly Pear without fail once a week. The girl who pretended nothing mattered, and the world didn't need to revolve around her or even notice how her eyes turned sad when she thought no one was looking.

Jessa might think no one saw her the way she craved to be seen, but I did. Every damn moment, in the light or the dark.

She caught my eye. Ever since the first time I saw her. And now, I watched her from the shadows, knowing someday, she would be mine.

# CHAPTER 1

## JESSA

"Oh no, you are not doing this to me. I am the one in control here, buddy. Not you. No matter what you think, I control you. Mr. Alphahole," I muttered as I glared at the screen of my MacBook. "And you *will* not derail me yet again. Even if you are such a swoon worthy, sexy daddy of a MMC that I wish could magically pop into existence."

My sigh, heavy and not at all the bad assery me I flung out into the unsuspecting world earlier, did nothing to deter the damn man in my next book.

Stolen Kisses.

I grinned, still loving the title, but not at all sure where the fuck I was going with the storyline.

Which was so unlike me.

Delena Bennett never did anything without a fully plotted and not pantsed storyline written in pencil in case *she* (which was me, of course) decided it needed a rerouting worthy of the GPS app on my phone. But, Liam, the man I was still trying to wrangle, refused to fucking cooperate.

He was being a Grade A dickwad, and while alphahole

sold, dickwad did not. And hell if I knew how to get him to heel.

Fucking men even screwed me over when I wrote them now. I glared at the keys, wishing for the hundredth time that for once, the beginning of the damn book would flow. But I had a sinking feeling that unlike my other novels, Liam was going to fuck me over.

Especially since I dished out for the guy from that damn stranded on an island TV show with the host I would climb.

Fuck, maybe I should just jump head first into a MFM and live out my late night fantasy. Host hottie would fulfill my age gap trope. But since the photo cost me more than I'd cared to admit out loud, sexy not winner of said stranded on an island man it was.

Reverse harem would have to wait. Mercilessly, I wrangled Liam into some semblance of acceptable asshole and quit before the urge to put the fucker in a scary Halloween mask really derailed my writing process.

Fucking viral videos had me second-guessing my kinks. And lane.

Only one thing would save me now. Outside, a steady rain had begun to fall, coating the streets in a silvery sheen that glistened and turned the world magical.

Well, at least the kind of magical that made my heart sing with all the quiet and stillness a rainy night brought.

With any luck, I'd get a decent night's sleep after, too.

Five minutes later, black Mary Poppins umbrella in hand, phone in my pocket, I stepped out into the night. For a moment, I dropped the umbrella and let the rain pepper my face in its sweet embrace. All the cares and stress melted away.

For a moment, the stress, worries, and silly loneliness disappeared.

Rain fell in a steady rhythm, never slowing and always

there as I walked the dimly lit neighborhood. Not for the first time, the back of my neck prickled with awareness.

I should have been scared. The fact crossed my mind more than once, my common sense trying to convince me that something sinister lurked in the shadows. But the other part of me, the one I let run free and created the book boyfriends I imagined, smiled a secret smile. Full of comfort, safety, and maybe a tiny rush that someone *was* watching me.

From the shadows.

Fucking imagination took off into directions I definitely could not follow, even I wanted to. As much as my walks in the rain made the loneliness disappear, the temporary reprieve lasted only as long as drops that fell.

But maybe, I could hold onto the feeling long enough to write a world where the girl didn't end up alone, surrounded by love. Love that, yes, I envied, but also made me realize the hole in my heart might never be filled the way I wanted.

*A girl could dream*, I thought, umbrella twirling in my grip.

# CHAPTER 2

## TY

"Pick up the pace, QB," I teased half heartedly, and grinned as Sebastian flipped me off. Our usual after-hours practice turned into a full on offensive line bonding session the last few weeks since our insane win without a damn kicker. The Fury weren't the bumbling idiots everyone thought we were going to be once the new owners took over.

Okay, so it was mostly the few asshole media wannabes saying it, but still, a guy had his pride.

"I know, number one in your heart." I winked. "Don't worry, I'll keep it our little secret. Maddie will never find out. As long as you promise to call me honey bear." I sprinted past my QB as he shot me another patented Lockwood glare.

"There's seriously something wrong with you, Ty," he grumbled as I shot out of reach.

"You still love me."

"Will the two of you knock it the fuck off before I lose my damn lunch," Handers complained, only half serious. "My wife thinks we spend too much time together as it is, and if she heard the two of you, she'd never let that shit go."

The whistle of Damon Ward, Fury physio health healer extraordinaire and former Olympic gold medalist to the extreme, interrupted me before I could respond. I grinned and ran to where the Gatorade sat as the other guys joined in. Sebastian leaned over, stretching like he always did after a run. My QB kept his body in prime shape, and worked his ass off.

I grabbed an extra cup and brought it to him as Damon made his way across the practice field.

The other guys who started showing up for extra time on the green circled up, the energy palpable.

That win was the catalyst for a season that no one would soon forget.

And this right here was the reason why.

"Delilah is going to get a few of you started on your somatic stretches, and then you're done," he said and shot a look at Sebastian, who looked like he was going to protest. "Rest is just as important, Lockwood."

"I tell him that, but he never listens."

"Shut the fuck up, Ty," Sebastian returned, but grinned at me.

"Taco night," I whooped, and Sebastian just shook his head, still smiling.

The guy smiled more now than in the entire two years I had known him in Cleveland. I'd like to take the credit, but Maddie deserved it. Hell, *he* deserved it. Guy worked harder than anyone I ever knew, except me, of course, and hid his heart under the guise of asshole.

But that being chipped away I took credit for.

In fact, I'd gladly take credit for the gooey mess he'd become because of Maddie.

After all, I was pretty fucking insistent my agent, Kellan Horne, find a way to get him signed to the Fury. And here we were. If not for me, QB would have never have spent weeks driving past Magpie Dreams and watching Maddie through the window.

Or ogling her at the Prickly Pear while eating his fucking weight in Pom Guac. Just the thought made my stomach rumble in anticipation. Fuck, those damn tacos were better than just about everything, except winning and playing with the team.

And *her*.

I thought about the bag of Darrell Lea Australian Licorice I left on her bed last night before she got home from her walk in the rain.

My mind immediately started going through what she would be doing right now, and it took everything in me not to sprint for the fucking door just so I could be there when she walked in. Watch her as her eyes lit up as she ordered her usual.

Pom Guac, Sweet Corn taco, Got Have It taco, and a Sweet Heat taco, dragon fruit marg extra lime. Plus seasonal mango pico the last few weeks.

And then again, I'd have to watch the damn bartender make her drink extra strong, because he knew just how she liked it.

I did, too, but that wasn't all I knew.

"Somats, shower, then food."

"Never thought I'd love a damn foam roller so much," one of the guys muttered as he headed toward Delilah, the newest member of the Fury training staff.

Damon introduced a joint and mobility based training regiment based on each player's position when he took over in the beginning of the season. At first, the guys grumbled until Coach made it abundantly clear it was a fall in line situation. Two months later, just about everyone stopped bitching about change once the hard work they were putting in off the field started paying off on the game side of ball.

QB's not so overt team building efforts added to it?

Fucking magic.

Shit was hard, no doubt, but the program guaranteed game day results on top of being able to walk like a normal person as the seasons piled up. But, forty-five minutes later, the good type of sore sat on my body like a warm blanket. Hell yes.

One minute closer to seeing her. Watching her. The way her eyes closed in bliss as she devoured her favorite things. The flush in her cheeks after a few drinks. Her tongue when it darted out to moisten her lips or her laughter as it drifted to my ears.

"Dude, the firecracking about the hours, move shower time so we can close up shop," Xavier, the defensive back the team acquired from LA, nudged my shoulder said, knocking me off kilter and out of my reverie.

"I smell better than most of these guys," I muttered. I extended my hand to Sebastian, who was sprawled out on the ground glaring at me. Seconds ticked as he regarded my hand as if it would bite him. "So I can catch your passes, but you won't let me help you up? Come one, tacos and Pom Guac await." I raised my brow until he let me haul him up. "And your girl. Lucky man. Best threesome ever."

"I hate that you know that," he grumbled as I chuckled.

"Naw, you love me. One day you'll say it out loud, and we'll have to assure Maddie our bromance will never interfere with your epicity."

"Not sparkling as an actual factual word!" Xavier called as he left the training area.

"Pshaw," I scoffed as I waved a dismissive hand in his direction. "Compared to the shit I've head him spew, that was fucking Shakespeare."

"Sometimes I need a damn translator for the guy," he added. "Bad enough I have to deal with you, but now this shit? Thank God he's on the D." My mouth opened, ready to spout a smart ass comment, but QB stopped me with his hand. "No comment, Simmons. No comment."

My laughter echoed through the hall as I slapped him on the back, but my blood buzzed at the prospect of seeing her again, and what she wore. If she had changed her shampoo or picked out a new shower gel.

Fuck. Yes.

# CHAPTER 3

## JESSA

"Oh, hell no, Mister I'm-going-ravage-you," I muttered, with a glare tossed in for good measure, at the screen of my laptop. Fingers tapped away as I waited for Reid and Maddie to finish unpacking the shipment Adam, our usual delivery guy, dropped off this morning.

The two of them rarely resisted the urge to rip open the boxes as soon as they arrived. Poor Adam might lose an arm one of these days. Then again, patience has never been one of my virtues, but I do love a long, drawn out wait. The expectation. The build.

The final release of all the built up tension and thoughts and…

Shit. I really needed to get laid.

Sigh.

From the way Adam tried to catch my eye when Reid snatched the boxes out his arms, I was fairly certain I'd have no problem getting him to help me take care of my overly active libido. Only problem?

Adam, as gorgeous as he was, and I'm talking cover model

ready, he did absolutely nothing to my lady parts. My inner whore pretty much turned her nose up at him, even while begging me to find a damn orgasm with something other than my right hand or my rechargeable boyfriends. It was like my body just ignored the fact that a get out of celibacy jail free card stood before me at least three times a week.

One year.

One year without feeling the warmth of a man's bare chest against my tits or his hands running along my naked body. My back, the dip of my spine…shit.

My fingers flew across the keyboard as I swiftly decided my inner whore would just have to make do with the fantasy spinning in my head.

Who says a girl had to *know or see* the guy giving her the big O? At this point, I'd take one of those crazy ass masked dudes my not-so-fellow authors of all things dark romance wrote about to help me get off.

"If I don't get a damn taco and a margarita in the next twenty minutes, I might faint from malnourishment," Maddie whined as her purse made a loud thud as she sat it on the counter next to me. My heart jumped into my throat as I slammed my laptop closed, praying to fucking God she didn't see what I'd been writing. Don't get me wrong, I knew the intimate details of both their damn love lives, and while the kinkiness of my bff's were anything but vanilla, I seriously doubted they'd understand the masked man I'd been considering.

Not to mention neither of them knew who Delena Bennett was. Or that I was her.

Mid level, semi best selling romance author of all things smut and kink loving with a huge dash of the feels thrown in.

There was no way I'd ever tell them, either. I'd never want them to think I'd share or write about anything they told me.

Even if there was a little praise kink, daddy Dom energy floating around my last few books.

This one, however, was being a huge asshole and making me nuts.

The damn fictional men in my life were being more of a pain in the ass than the ones in my real life. Both nonexistent and not attracted to in the least realsies.

Her brow furrowed. "You ok?"

I nodded quickly, sliding my laptop into its case. "Just checking emails and making sure there's nothing else to follow up on before we lock up. Anything good in the shipment?"

Her eyes lit up, and let out an inner sigh of relief as she responded the way I'd hoped she would to my topic switch. "The blue Versace came, and Jessa, if my boobs looked like yours, I'd probably have to get a second job, no wait, third job to pay for it. Because it's even more stunning in person. It needs a little repair, but nothing that should affect the integrity, thankfully." Her phone pinged, and she grinned. "In fact, Reid and I think you should add it to your collection."

"First," I held up a finger, "Sebastian would buy it for you just so you wouldn't have to get a third job." Next finger. "And your second job is even better than your first. Third," I let out a dramatic sigh, "I'd have to get a damn kitten just so *someone* would see me in it. That dress deserves an audience, at least from one other person, and sadly, there are no prospects in sight as of," I studied my watch, "ten seconds ago. Nor do I predict any change in that status in the near future."

"There's a guy who would take you out in a hot second, if you'd just looked his way," Reid said in a singsong voice as she came in from the back, eyes twinkling like she had a plan up her sleeve.

I stopped her before she could get another word out.

"While I appreciate your meddlesome ways, keeping the Lockwood brothers waiting is *never* a good idea. Even if you like your ass spanked," She glared, then let out a giggle. I turned my attention to Maddie. "Or have multiple orgasms all damn night. So leave me to my damn tacos. And my dragon fruit marg. And my book boyfriends. They do it better."

Maddie and Reid both burst out laughing. Reid added as I glared while we grabbed our things and headed to the door of Magpie Dreams, "Oh, Jessa. One day, you're going to find your own Tall, Dark, and Cinnastalker."

"I can't believe you still remember that term," I muttered, turning the key in the lock.

"And I can't believe you don't believe in HEA's, given Drunk Book Club."

"Drunk Book Club exists *because* of HEA's. Of course I believe." With a roll of my eyes and a smirk, I looped my arms through theirs as we made our way to the Prickly Pear. "My besties both got theirs, and that's all I need."

"My DBC's!" Nicky, our favorite waitress and co-owner of the Prickly Pear along with her big brother Frankie nearly bounced with excitement as we made our way to our favorite table.

Drunk Book Club. Yep, Nicky totally hit up the last Drunk Book Club meeting two weeks ago, armed with Pom Guac and take out from the Prickly Pear…and Rhett's, the adorable new bartender, number. Drunk Book Club has gone from two to six. Sometimes, Kylie, Reid's older sister, came with Alex and Gia if their schedules didn't conflict. Kylie owned an open wheel racing team, and Alex's dad was

Bobby Anders, the famous racecar driver turned team owner. She and Gia both worked for Anders Racing.

Sigh.

My editor loved sending me reminders that holding out for book boyfriends meant real life men would never meet the standards I created. Duh. But, then again, she didn't see my friend's amazing relationships.

I seriously think it might be a Lockwood brother thing. It has to be in the genes, even they both had their issues that almost messed up their HEA's. Love persevered. Reid and Maddie deserved all the happiness, and orgasms, the Lockwood brothers gave them. Separately, of course.

Or whatever. Who was I to judge? Some of the things I wrote would have the pearl-clutchers making the sign of the cross while they looked for lightning to strike me down.

*Cheers, bitches*, I thought as I took the dragon fruit margarita Nicky handed me as I perched on my mismatched barstool. "Sweet elixir of Thursday night happiness, I have missed you!" My eyes closed in ecstasy (hey, a girl needs her moment when the Big O is a one hand buzz event). "Tell Rhett thank you."

"Oh, he didn't-"

"How's my girl?" Sebastian Lockwood, Carolina Fury quarterback murmured as he swept Maddie into his arms. I delicately rolled my eyes while Reid pretended to peek through her fingers before dissolving into laughter as they kissed.

Mr. Tall, Dark, and not-so-Asshole anymore made Maddie's eyes shine in a way they hadn't as long as I'd known her. It was enough to convince me, and everyone in The Prickly Pear, he loved her more than anything in the world.

Even football. Though, I was pretty sure it came in a close second. The Fury were having one hell of a season. Or so I'd been told. Football wasn't something I'd followed much beyond going to a game here and there if invited. But those family suite tickets were making a fan out of me despite my best intentions.

"Public displays of affection, while adorable, are not recommended on an empty taco or margarita stomach," I muttered good naturedly as I took a generous and well earned sip of my favorite tequila spiked concoction. A forty-five hundred word count day deserved Prickly Pear's finest deliciousness. I glanced over the rim of my marg to see Ty Simmons, Sebastian's best friend and tight end for the Fury, dipping a tortilla chip into *my* Pom Guac and mango pico.

The special menu edition Frankie, Prickle Pear's owner, added on just for the season.

And I planned on consuming as much of it as humanly possible. Let Sebastian and Maddie have the regular Pom Guac.

Me? I wanted the good stuff. Especially since the two of them were bumping uglies and having multiple orgasm nights while I wrote about dominant alphaholes who might just end up wearing a mask of some sort.

If I ever got over the night Kevin Reynolds forced me to watch Scream with him freshman year of college because he was convinced it would get him laid if I was freaked out.

Spoiler alert. I wasn't. And he didn't. Guy had a tongue like a jackhammer and almost made me throw up he was shoving it in my mouth so hard.

Yeah, that mask definitely had bad memories attached. I sighed, wondering how I was going to make the masked alphahole work when Ty dipped yet another chip into my treasure trove of smooth, savory sweet goodness.

I smacked his hand with a glare. "Hey there, cinnamon roll, get your own. This is all mine," I crooned as I pulled the bowl out of his reach with a grin. He blinked, then glanced from my hand to my face, his mouth twitching on one side. I narrowed my eyes at him. "Don't think your cute smile and puppy dog eyes will sway me, buddy. This is all mine. I don't share."

He blinked again, this time slower, and something flashed quickly behind his eyes. But it disappeared before I could name it. "QB, be right back. Maddie's friend might take my arm off if I don't get my own." His hand tapped the table, and he turned, but not before adding, "I only share once in a while. And even then, it comes with a price."

Before I could answer or even try to figure out what he meant, he walked away. "What the fuck did that mean?"

Sebastian shrugged as he ate a mouthful of regular Pom Guac from the huge bowl Nicky had set in between him and Maddie. "I've seen him keep the ball from defenders in a way most guys would never be able to do in a million years. But when it comes to food, especially here? Asshole made me watch the damn Notebook and then the After movie for accidentally eating his takeout instead of mine. Twice."

"Ah, a renaissance man," I nodded, still not sure why the comment unsettled me. I shook my head, clearing out the Ty Simmons confusion cobwebs and downed the margarita.

"There are so few of those left," Reid said wistfully as she toyed with the small gold padlock charm around her neck.

"What? No Tall, Dark, and Daddy tonight?"

Her mouth turned down as she pouted for a moment then straightened her shoulders. "Owen had a last minute client emergency. He flew out this morning, but he'll be home tomorrow. Or else," she added.

"Ooh, trouble in BDSM paradise?" I asked with a grin. Her cheeks flushed, and cackled.

"We had plans," she said, and her eyes widened a fraction as she let out a small squeak.

"What is wrong with you?"

"Nothing," she muttered, cheeks turning bright red.

Nicky slid in between us as she sat down another dragon fruit marg in front of me. Reid shifted on the stool. "I didn't order another yet-"

The perky waitress shrugged. "I was told to keep one in your hand, and to bring more of this. I'm a good girl, remember?" She winked and I giggled and put more mango pico down in front of me.

Yep. Yet another kink test victim.

"Tell Frankie thank you-"

She opened her mouth, but Ty chose that moment to return to the table, a huge bowl of his own treasured guac in hand. "Nice to see you smile after that practice, QB."

"Big game, right?"

Sebastian nodded at Reid. "Yep. Wild Card. Win or lose, best damn season I've had in a long time."

"Aw, shucks, you know you don't have to say that in front of your girl and her friends. We're in public and all," Ty joked, batting his eyes at Sebastian, who glared before a small smile snuck its way onto his chiseled features. The man could cut granite with those cheekbones.

Sigh.

"I swear, Simmons, one day it's going to be serious fucking payback."

With a grin, Ty snorted over a mouthful of taco. He swallowed before saying, "One day might never come."

"What might never come?" Reid asked, delicately taking a bite of her own food.

Sebastian answered, arm looped around Maddie's waist as she pulled her closer. "Girlfriend."

The tall and if I had to admit it, gloriously built tight end rolled his eyes. "You know you're all I need.'"

Finger pointed at him, Sebastian returned, "That's

because you eat, drink, and dream football. But, one day, it'll happen. All that focus will find another place to land on."

His eyes glanced around the room and fell on the bar, where Rhett was wiping down the counter. "Focus never changes QB. Just finds another thing you can't live without."

# CHAPTER 4

## TY

*F*uck, she smelled good.

Not that I didn't know exactly how she smelled. From her shower gel, shampoo, conditioner, hair treatments and body spray, not a single part of Jessa's daily routine went unnoticed by me.

Even if I could only watch her in the morning before practice or my workout, then late at night when she worked late at Magpie Dreams or on the rare occasion she had a night off, I saw it all.

And watching her tonight across the table, it took everything in me not to remind Rhett and Frankie who they were no longer allowed to look at. But, the extra tip I slipped him along with a firm yet gentle reminder I could easily kick his ass if he didn't get the message worked wonders on the guy's eyesight.

The way she puckered her lips after the first taste made visions of her on her knees, those luscious lips wrapped around my cock as her eyes begged me to do all the things that would make her wet. Tears and the choking noises she would make as my cock hit the back of her throat without mercy. My beautiful Wildfire would want it all, and more. Her pussy just waiting to be filled the way her throat was, taking every damn inch and thrust I gave her.

*Fuck.*

Gray eyes that stole the soul from my body the first time they locked on mine. The Universe itself stood still, and suddenly, all the work and effort I put into football felt like a damn warm up for the big show.

Jessa.

When Sebastian started following Maddie home work, I was sure my carefully laid plans at winning and building a team with the one guy I knew could bring his A game no matter what were shot to shit. But, then I saw *her* and I understood.

So I helped the one guy who never gave me shit about the way I had to fold my damn towel before I took a shower. Or the number of reps I did had to hit a certain number on the clock or count in my head.

Who saw my focus on the game and playing it the best I fucking could as a good thing. And accepted that I was a part of his life because he was how I wanted to play the game.

We needed each other.

But I never thought I'd need someone like her.

QB was my best friend, and fuck, he was too fun to tease. Seeing him happy, and knowing it was the final piece he needed to be at his best made it easier for me to breathe. To focus and play the game. Train. Put in the work.

Then my world flipped upside fucking down.

Breathing became at once easier and harder than it had ever been.

I needed to know her. Her likes. Dislikes. The way she brushed her hair, or how she slept late at night, all alone. Curled up around a pillow or sprawled out like the entire bed was her oasis.

How she liked her coffee, or what she watched when she was sad or felt alone.

And most of all, how she looked when she lost control. When she let herself shatter as she touched herself, climaxing with wild abandon.

From across the bar at the Prickly Pear, she became the other focal point in my world.

So I made sure QB got the girl, made up with his brother, and rallied the entire team to get behind him. Of course, fate stepped in a few times, but I'd like to think those three crazy bitches liked how I handled some things.

The fates or divine intervention could only go so far.

My brain started working out a list of all the things I needed to know about her in the few seconds she turned and let her eyes slide down my body that first night.

Secrets, darkest desires. Simplest moments of happiness.

I needed each and every one.

Now? She couldn't hide a single thing from me. Ever again.

I grinned as I pulled out the phone I purchased earlier today. No way in hell was I going to take a chance that she'd figure out who I was before I was ready.

The cooler than usual for this time of year night air did nothing to calm down the party wanting to happen in my pants as I tapped out a quick message and hit the arrow on the right of the text.

> A bit late to be researching, don't you think?

Two weeks ago, I found out Jessa's secret.

She wrote spicy as fuck romance under the pen name Delena Bennett.

Vampire Diaries fan. Not quite as dark and twisted as some of the books out there, but enough to tell me she had all kinds of pent-up frustration she worked out when she put words to paper, or laptop.

At first, I read her books hoping to figure out how to get an edge. But, damn, she could write. Edgy but not something that caused my eyes to roll in disbelief.

I wasn't stupid enough to think just because she wrote it, she wanted it. In fact, I could tell she worked out her frustrations and dreams, and hell, her loneliness by writing.

Loneliness I recognized. It was easy to be in a room filled with people and still feel alone. For years, the game became the only thing I cared about. Hours of watching tape, learning plays, pushing my body to its limit. Working out until my body couldn't take anymore.

Head down, end game in mind. But nobody saw me. I didn't let them.

I couldn't let anything get in the way of achieving the goals I set for myself. The ones I knew would make my dad proud. Football and going to games were all I had with him once my parents divorced. The game quickly grew into the one thing we had that was ours. The hours I spent were all for him. The two weekends a month we spent together.

No friends. Girlfriends that lasted longer than a few months. Not because I wanted to stick my dick into someone else.

Football meant everything, and anything or anyone who distracted me from it, I cut out.

And that fucking day I watched as QB stuck around and added extra practice I knew he had the same determination I did. Thank fuckI left my phone in the locker room and had to go back and get it. He loved the game for his own reasons, but it was there. Despite the fact the rest of the team thought he was a complete asshole. To be fair, he was. On the outside. But anyone who puts that much time, effort, and sure force of will into something hides things, good and bad. Underneath it all, Sebastian Lockwood had good and not so bad in spades, hidden away from the world.

Those workouts soon became the only place I breathed easier.

Did I really want to date him? Maybe. Bromances were made on flimsier excuses. Me and QB?

Fucking dynasty in the making. Guy was my other half on the field.

All I needed. Until I saw her.

And the world righted itself one more time.

Just like the game I loved, I had to learn everything about her.

> Jessa: It's never too late. For a...little research.

*2:32 am*

I threw an arm over my eyes, the sheets twisted around my body. Brain racing as it went over the playbook for this week's game. Ran every play, remembering the weaknesses in Florida's D. This game would either turn the tide, or be the end of it all. But the upcoming game wasn't what really had me up at fucking two am.

It was her. My Wildfire.

My fingers twitched with the need to *do* something. I squinted in the darkness, fumbling as I felt the bed for the extra phone I fell asleep holding only a few hours before.

The screen lit up, still on the messaging app I used earlier.

Jessa's pen name drew me in like a moth the most beautiful flame I'd ever fucking laid eyes on.

I chuckled in the darkness, the room only lit by the

moonlight filtering in from the window across from my bed. I bet no one figured out she was a Vampire Diaries fan.

Or maybe they had. But I was the only one who linked it to Jessa. Her lowkey obsession with binge watching first thing in the morning while she had her coffee and got ready.

Fucking show almost made me late for team workout a few times, but damn, I couldn't stop watching each expression as it crossed her face. From the smirk, the swooning sighs, and fuck, even when she cried whenever Damon showed his vulnerable side.

I grinned, remembering how pissed she was over her mango pico. Fuck, she was beautiful. Storms in her eyes, the fire in her words. When she snatched it from me, my cock went from maybe to fuck yes. Damn zipper almost killed me.

> Jessa: It's never too late. For a…little research.

My palm slid down my stomach and grazed the full-on salute in my boxer briefs as I reread her response from earlier as she left the Prickly Pear.

The way her eyes widened a fraction as she realized who messaged her. One side of her mouth lifted in a secret smile, fingers flying as she tapped out her response, lips parted.

Still researching, Wildfire?

Moments ticked by in silence. Maybe my intuition about her sleep schedule was wrong. *Maybe she did fall into a deep sleep after all that mango pico,* I thought with a smirk as I pictured her eyes closed in bliss as she took bite after bite.

But, then, the dots started moving.

> Jessa: Always. What, can't sleep? Need a good book 2 read ;)

> Thought you might be up. I've read them all, Wildfire.

Seconds ticked by as I pictured her nose scrunched up as she contemplated my message.

I wasn't lying. The minute I found out what Jessa hid from the rest of the world, I read each and every one of her books. Cover to cover.

Fucking Kindle app killed the dead time at practice and cool down sessions. No one knew I was reading some of the spiciest (thanks, Booktok) romance I never knew existed until Delena Bennett walked into my life.

Or, when Maddie walked into Sebastian's life and I dragged him to the Prickly Pear after finding out he drove by Magpie Dreams just to catch a glimpse of her. Thank fucking God the two of them were best friends.

A guy had to watch out for his circle, and hack away at the chip on Sebastian's shoulder to help him figure out Maddie was it? Ten times more difficult if they weren't best friends.

Because Jessa embedded herself into my being instantly and in a way nothing else, even football, had.

> Jessa: Crazy stalker fan, then? Should I be worried?

> Fan? I like the term admirer.

> Jessa: Secret? Or not so secret?

> Whatever you like, Wildfire.

Her fingers typed out a response and then stopped. The process repeated a few times, and I held a breath, wondering what the hell she was thinking.

I knew what I was thinking. Because I knew what she liked. Fuck, sometimes I felt like a creeper after I walked by her place one night and caught her in bed. Curtains barely opened. I only saw it because a car sped down her normally quiet street and I was afraid she'd see me. So, I made a fucking dash for the side of her house. Granted, the houses had tall arborvitae trees for privacy and enough space so that it wasn't the peeping Tom from the other house you had to worry about.

Nope, only guys like me, hiding so no one would recognize me, lurking in the shadows. Pretending to take a late night stroll in a neighborhood that was not mine, looking in the window of a girl who had no clue I was the guy she kept her guac from with the cutest glare and the guy she messaged. Skirted the line with, anonymous and safe,

> Jessa: What if I am not sure what I like? What if there are things I'd like to try, to see if I like them?

Are you asking for help, Wildfire?

I held my breath, my ready to go buddy in my briefs more eager than I cared to admit as I watched my messenger sit, blank, waiting to see how and if she responded.

> Jessa: Why? Do you know of anyone who might be willing to help a spicy romance author out?

Fuck. Me. Sideways.

Looking for a research partner, Wildfire?

> Jessa: Depends on if the research partner felt like he could participate in the type of research only a spicy AF romance writer would need to do. Very hard to come by.

The split second the words appeared, images of Jessa in every filthy fantasy I'd had the last two months played out in flashes that made me almost come on the spot.

> Hard? Freudian slip, Wildfire? Because it is definitely hard, but not the way that would make me not apply for the position.

From past experience, I could picture the way her eyes narrowed, nose scrunched. Adorable, sexy as fuck, and everything that made it so fucking hard for me not to go to her right this fucking second.

> Jessa: Think of it as a job qualification. Necessary skill in order to pursue the research in question.

The line we were skating blurred even more with every late night conversation, hiding behind anonymity that was becoming less and less anonymous. The lines become more blurry with each message. Every teasing exchange, the intensity of how much I fucking wanted her. How her words, the things she said made it harder and harder not to do all the things I'd fantasized about.

My cock twitched, wanting her. Needing her.

> What kind of research are we talking? Just to know if I have the necessary skills to be adequately qualified for the position.

> Jessa: The position would be flexible, of course. The need to be able to slightly or drastically depending on the position needed.

*If only she knew how many positions I fantasized about, she'd hire me on the spot,* I thought.

> Mildly interested. What type of research will it require beyond being able to adjust to ensure you're satisfied with the current activity?

Worried I took it too far, I almost sent an apology when my fucking jaw nearly hit the floor, my cock begged so hard that I was on the edge of coming just from what I read.

My phone pinged with a picture of Jessa, neck down, wearing a lacy bra and panty, a sheet partly covering her thick thighs. My mouth watered, cock finally breaking out of its confines and peaking out from the waistband of my damn briefs..

And then...

> Jessa: How do you feel about wearing a mask?

# CHAPTER 5

## TY

*Four months ago...*
"There's no such thing as too big, Mads."

The sexiest voice I'd ever heard called out over the din of the happy hour/dinner crowd at my favorite place in town, and my cock immediately stood at attention.

Fuck.

A bolt of pleasure shot down my spine as a purely animalistic voice in my head growled *MINE* without seeing who the voice belonged to.

Her.

Frankie tipped his chin as QB and I made our way through the crowd at the Prickly Pear. Nicky, his little sister and the hardest working person in this damn town, would be around with my order. I flashed him two fingers, because there was no way in hell I'd be sharing any of my taco goodness or the damn Pom Guac.

Stuff was as addictive as scoring a touchdown against the GOAT right before the clock ticked down to OT.

No doubt, Sebastian was going to lose his mind over it, just like the girl he was pining over did every damn week. If his reaction to seeing her through the store window told me anything, he was going to freak the fuck out when he saw the face she made when she ate the guac from heaven.

Fate intervened when I decided to catch a glimpse of the girl who occupied the non-football moments in my head, even though there was a chance she might see me and recognize me before I could disappear, even with the storm moving in. My place was on the way to Lockwood's, and when he stopped in front of Magpie Dreams and he couldn't take his eyes off the girl in the window, I knew right then and there I had to step in and give fate a little nudge in the right direction.

It didn't hurt that she frequented the Prickly Pear with *her* as much as I did.

Yep, might've been coming here for a few weeks, even before training camp began.

Fucking win-win. Because the BFF of the girl I had been watching and obsessing over since the first happy hour and heavenly tacos, was the same from QB's drive-by.

I canted my head to the side, just enough to catch sight of stormy gray eyes scanning the crowd, full lips parted as she did that wag your finger thing girls did when they saw someone they knew. A growl escaped my lips before I could stop it.

"If you're that hungry, you can have it all," Sebastian grumbled as he reached for a chip.

Nicky winked as she finished unloading the tray of tacos, chips, salsas, Pom Guac, and two domestics and then left us to deliver more deliciousness to the waiting masses.

"Nope, brought you here, plan on getting you addicted so I don't look like some creeper who comes in here by himself every damn Thursday." I handed him a foil wrapped piece of heaven with a grin. "Never say I don't treat you right, QB."

"Just as long as you don't tell anyone we're dating," he

muttered, but I saw the flash of something he tried to hide since that first time we worked out together.

Hell. Yes. I was growing on him, weaseling my way in his heart.

Bromance central.

"You know you love me, but don't worry, I'll keep it between us," I teased as I grabbed my phone off the high pub-style table and sent off a quick message.

> If you keep posting pics of tacos, I might just have to find you one day.

Sebastian just glared, but his face contorted in ecstasy when he took a bite of the taco in his hand. "Holy fuck."

I nodded at the Pom Guac. "Try that, QB."

> Jessa: Oh, a taco lover?

The taco I just shoved happily into my mouth nearly came out as I choked on it. Fuck yeah I was. Especially when I didn't have to order it off a damn menu.

> Damn, Wildfire. Not sure you understand how fucking true that statement is. How's the writing going?

Out of the corner of my eye, I watched her sneak into the hallway that led to the bathrooms and a few storage rooms. Dimly lit and private, that damn hallway played out in a few of the fantasies I had about Jessa ever since the first time she walked through the door of the Prickly Pear.

I nearly choked on my taco then, too. Only my third day in town before training camp began in two weeks. My plan to get QB signed to the Fury in full swing. Focused on the season, my team, and building a dynasty.

Gray eyes, long waves of dark hair that looked like fucking chocolate brownies covered in dark chocolate ganache. I fucking loved those. Full tits, tall enough that my head could rest on the top of hers. But what made my cock harder than a fucking field goal attempt without a damn kicker?

The fire and sass she exuded, yet looked so alone without even knowing she wasn't going to be ever again.

I called in a few favors with a hacker friend of mine from home back in Cleveland who turned legit not too long ago, and Dante helped me brush up on my skills from school since playing professional ball meant no more stupidity that could land my ass in jail. Or worse.

One rainy night, I walked by her house, and a car scared the shit out of me, so I hid behind a tree as it sped down the street and took the corner, tires squealing.

Through the window, I watched as Jess sat on an oversized chair, typing away at a laptop that sat atop her criss crossed knees, blanket around her shoulders.

Nose wrinkling in concentration, she reached for a bag, and pulled out a few pieces of candy.

That's when I recognized the familiar brown paper bag colored sack filled with the one candy I couldn't resist.

Darrell Lea Australian licorice.

That I ordered in bulk online because no one around here sold it.

Fate.

My overactive imagination imagined all kinds of scenarios with Jessa, naked, me, teasing her with the tiny pieces. Kissing her and tasting her after she had a few pieces. Doing all kinds of filthy things with it so I could taste her on a few pieces.

When she snapped a picture of the bag with her phone

and then typed away a few things, I assumed she posted it on either Magpie's account or her personal one. But the only thing on Magpie's grid were pictures of Reid, the store owner in some dress, and nothing on hers.

I nearly gave up, until I did a location search plus the brand name of the licorice.

And then, I found her social media accounts attached to an account online and nearly fell out of my chair.

Jessa was a spicy romance author. And not just any. She wrote some kinky, sexy shit with storylines that I couldn't fucking put down.

And like the creeper I was starting to feel like, I hacked one of Dante's sleeper accounts so I could manipulate it. Nothing freaked people out more than a new account suddenly following them. The Fury had a social media manager who took over the one I had as soon as I signed my contract, and I had never been more happy to not deal with it.

Two posts in five months was my damn limit.

But now, I had a fucking reason to have an online presence. I set up various pics of me traveling, no face, ambiguous and non threatening. Not even five minutes after I had it set up and followed her, D texted me.

> Dante: Hey, T. Next time you need a sneaker, just tell me. Good luck with your girl.

> Roger, D. Keep U updated.

At first, I sent one message, asking her where she found the candy because I was having a hard time finding it in my area. Of course, my account said I lived about an hour or so away from hers, and I'd hoped she'd take the bait.

> That licorice is everything. Just moved and can't find it anywhere. Care to share where you found it?

She didn't respond for a few days, but when she did, I nearly fucking jumped for joy in the middle of my leg session in the Fury training center. QB gave me the side eye, and Xavier, fresh off the IR, nodded like he shared a secret with me.

> Jessa: There is a store that carries imported candy and hand-crafted chocolate. They order it for me every few weeks. I can get you the name? My favorite indulgence.

I sent a thumbs up, not wanting to scare her away. Plus I knew she was the store QB's estranged brother, Owen's, girlfriend owned. Oh, the twisted webs we weave.

After that, I sent her a few messages here and there, and after the owner at the Sweet Indulgences Shoppe ordered my case, I thanked her and told her I hoped I could control myself enough to make it last more than a few days.

A few messages a day turned into *'Good Morning, Wildfire'* because she lit me on fire. She thought it was because her latest release hit the top 100 in the online giant she self published through.

The *'Sweet Dreams'* she sent turned into late night discussions about things she was writing, or my travels; which wasn't a lie, because we did play a few pre-season games, and I loved to travel in the off season. As long as I could still get my workouts in.

The two a.m. conversations we had while I watched her through her window became a twice a week habit. And when I watched her make herself come using a toy, I nearly broke down her damn door and made her orgasm again and again. With the toy and my cock.

I didn't mind a teammate, as long he knew his place.

And now? Things were getting to the point I wasn't sure I could hold back much longer.

Jessa was going to be mine. It was time to start showing her just how much I knew about her.

# CHAPTER 6

## JESSA

"Oh, God, Jessa, what the fuck are you doing?"

I buried my face in my hands as I plopped down on the couch in the middle of Magpie Dreams. I still had a half hour before Reid would be here, and Maggie had the day off, thank God.

Because I didn't know how much longer I could keep lying to the two of them.

Okay, maybe not lying. But omitting crazy, stalkery, if not sexy things from my two best friends, not to mention that I was DELENA FUCKING BENNETT, was wearing on my nerves.

Because this week at Drunk Book Club, we were discussing *my book*. The one with Cross the Line.. The ties. And the bondage. And the really dirty talk on top of the really dirty sex I wrote about. It was one thing to hear all about Reid and Owen's sex life, or Maddie and Sebastian's, and even then I knew they didn't give me all the details. But to think they were going to read all the crazy sometimes fantasies I had and wrote about and have to act ignorant?

There were not enough margs or bags of Australian licorice to get me through it.

Not to mention that I was pretty much flirting and borderline insanely considering stranger sex in the guise of 'research' for a book they didn't know I was writing.

I stood up so fast I nearly knocked over the coffee that I didn't have to order because it was waiting for me at the coffee shop that had the most delicious Death By Chocolate muffins paid for and piping hot.

Just the way I liked it. From *him.*

No doubt about it. I had a stalker? Admirer?

And I sent him that picture the other night, invited him like a freaking cat in heat to do crazy things like wear a mask and do… things in the name of *research?*

Yep. It was official. All this no sex was making me reckless, horny, and far too accepting of a situation that could go seriously wrong.

Fucking Australian licorice.

Add to it all, Reid, Maddie, and I were supposed to go to the Fury Wild Card game this weekend in New Orleans. Reid told us all we were going away for the weekend, no questions asked. Between DBC, the game, and Masked Hottie Fuck Me to get my writers block gone, I might just have to stick a damn needle in my vein for caffeine and forgo the ecstasy of caffeinated coffee concoctions.

The writer's block was such bullshit, too. I knew where the damn story was going. Masked hottie beats up the dickhead who tries to corner his girl in the hallway of the bar, and then he follows her home to make sure she's safe. But can't control his emotions, or the anaconda in his pants who needs to make sure she, and her vagina, are safe, so he breaks in, gets her consent, and they fuck like bunnies but hotter.

But I wasn't sure it worked. Did masks freak people out? And how the hell did consent get in the picture? Because what if the wrong guy breaks in? Then, what, do I suddenly have a reverse harem or touch her and die sitch?

"FUUUUUUUCK," I yelled to the empty store. Or so I thought.

"Should I wait outside, or do you want breakfast? Because Nicky made some crazy, delicious Pom Guac inspired breakfast sandwich on a jalapeño ciabatta with egg whites and other stuff I'm sure she told me, but I can't remember." Reid popped a hand on her hip, gorgeous and eyeing me with one hand on her hip and a brown paper handled bag wafting a scent that, even in my crazed state, made my mouth water.

I moaned, then made a grabbing motion with my hands. "Food, yes, please," I begged shamelessly in my love for anything Nicky concocted. Frankie might be the owner and bartending genius at the Prickly Pear, but everyone in town soon learned it was his baby sister's culinary masterpieces and imagination that made the place a hit.

She snatched the bag out of reach, and said, "But only if you spill."

The death glare I shot her failed miserably, so I relented. Collapsing into myself as I dropped back on the couch I said, "There's too much, and not enough time, Reid. And maybe we should postpone Drunk Book Club."

With a snort she handed me a wrapped sandwich-sized bundle. "Hell no. I have been waiting for this damn book to come out, and I *need* girl time to squeal all over it. Because poor Owen might never be able to get his ties to be the same ever again." Her eyes flashed and her wicked grin made me want to swear again.

At least someone was getting some because of my fantasies.

*You could totally get some masked hottie love,* the inner whore who dressed like a devil on my shoulder whispered loudly in my ear.

*What better way to figure out the consent than to try it out in real life?* The inner slut dressed like an angel who sat on my other shoulder countered.

Great. Now hussy Halloween fantasies were arguing about my masked man hottie. I tore open the paper and took a bite. "Holy fuck." My eyes nearly rolled into the back of my head from the flavors melting and exploding all over my tongue.

Reid made similar ecstasy-filled noises as he ate hers. Over a bite she whined, "I'm so sad she's leaving in a few weeks."

"Wait, what?"

She nodded. "Yep. Frankie and she are opening a second Prickly Pear in Love Beach. But it's going to be fusion, all her menu and craft margs with desserts," she lamented.

"But, who is going to do our tacos and make us moan with pure orgasmic yumminess if she isn't here?"

"Oh, there's a silver lining. Apparently Nicky has a friend, Angelia, from culinary school that needed a change of scenery and has been shadowing her, learning the menu. Plus, she has a brother who plays hockey. I think her last name is Hale?"

"Wait, as in Jacob Hale?"

"That's it! Yes!"

"Reid, Jacob Hale is the hot lumbersnack goalie for the Seattle Revenge."

Her nose wrinkled. "Lumbersnack?"

"Beard. Muscles. Hair shaved on the side, longish on the top. Big. Could split those damn tree chunks, or a watermelon, with his thighs. Butterfly warm-up stretches? Best save percentage in the league. He has a sister? Is she Viking-like, too?"

Eyes wide, she laughed. "Definitely not Viking. More like a tiny ball of energy that helped Nicky with these this morning. Interesting. We should totally start going to hockey games."

"Oh no, this football stuff needs to end first, because I am not closing Magpie for another sport until football season ends. But we should then, and until then, also enjoy it on your big ol' tall, dark and daddy's TV. And then-"

"I get it." She looked at the clock. "Almost time to open. Candace Ward is coming in with a few charity auction details for Kylie's charity event from clients at Fortress before our first consultation."

"It's months away, though?"

She shrugged, then toyed with the single ring necklace she wore every day without fail since Owen . "Kylie wants to get a few of the Fury players and their girlfriends or wives to walk with the drivers and the other women. Ooh, maybe we could get your lumbersnack in on the action!"

I tossed the empty bag and other trash in the basket behind the counter. "He's not *my* lumbersnack, but I'm so in."

Reid paused at the door to the back dressing area and lounge, one hand on the doorframe. "Don't think you got away with not spilling. Pre-DBC, understood?"

I rolled my eyes. "Fine. Yay Delena Bennett."

"You better have read it," she called from the back.

Sigh. Yep, I read it all right. And fantasized about it. Might've even made my mini figs from a Lego set my niece bought me from the last Marvel Movie to make sure the logistics worked out.

Fuck. My. Life.

∼

THE NEXT NIGHT, pre Drunk Book Club, the rain that fell dappled the streets with a shimmering, dream-like quality, so I decided to walk to Reid and Owen's place.

I let out a pitiful sigh. Even my damn inner monologue sounded like absolute shit. If I didn't get over this writer's block soon, I was liable to start sounding like Garrett Struthers when he wrote me a love poem in ninth grade. The prose was so bad that I hid in a locker once to avoid looking him in the face. Of course, the locker belonged to Archer Wolf, who I ended up losing my virginity to after prom a few months later.

Kismet.

But, that wasn't the damn point. I shivered, cursing myself for not grabbing my jacket before I left. Like a teenage boy who wore shorts in a blizzard, I foolishly thought the chunky sweater would keep me warm on the ten minute walk. My hands gripped the handle of the Mary Poppins umbrella tighter, the rain falling at a steady pace. And wished I had a magic carpet bag full of everything I'd never need instead of the tiny designer purse Reid gave me for Christmas..

Scratch that. I'll always want this purse. But I'd still love a magical bag that would have a jacket at this moment, too. At least the rain fell like one of those fancy rain shower heads. Exactly like the one I bought but never installed because I was terrified I'd fuck up and lose my shower time. There was nothing I loved more than a hot shower, a few sprigs of eucalyptus, and a glass of moscato.

And now I'm totally thinking of *him*. A figurative glance around to make sure no cars were coming before I drifted into some fantasy while crossing the street and ended up in a hospital bed with those anti-traction debacles from getting run over. Careful to tiptoe around the puddles and not get my boots all wet.

The first time he left a bag of Darrell Lea Australian licorice on my doorstep a month after we began talking freaked me out enough that I nearly called the police to file a report in case my body was never found. But after reading the handwritten attached, the warmth that spread along my body replaced any lingering doubts.

> *Sweet Indulgences Shoppe ordered me an extra bag, and when I mentioned that an author sent me their way, they knew who I meant right away. And offered to have one of their employees drop off the extra bag to you. Along with this note. I'm pretty sure three bags will last me at least a week, and it will give me an excuse to stop in for a few more things when I run out.*
>
> *From one Aussie L lover to another,*
> *A Meandering Man...*

A Meandering Man. Fuck. In my head, for the last two days, he was not meandering at all.

More like masked.

Not too many nights ago, I returned home after one of my walks in the rain, and found a bag on my bed. Confused as fuck because I didn't remember leaving it there. And I *always* know where I leave my candy. I quickly dismissed the crazy thoughts swirling like a hurricane in my head and jumped right into the eye of the storm.

The little devil who loved to encourage my inner whore to have all the fun fantasies, purely in the name of research, took advantage of my alone time with my favorite toy later that night, and started filling my head with all kinds of masked men fantasies.

Well, not all kinds of men. Just one. The man whose face I've never seen. But then again, he didn't know mine either.

Or did he?

From that moment on, or should I say from that explosive orgasm on, the scenario played out over and over in my head. Leading to the crazy DMs I sent asking for 'help' doing 'research'.

Reid's townhome was lit from within, the lights and Christmas decorations up until the middle of January for her grandmother. I sucked in a fortifying breath before rapping my knuckles on the heavy wooden door, smiling at her wreath with a huge ass red bow on it. I pushed open the door, knowing she left it unlocked for me even though Owen hated it when she did that.

No doubt, I'd hear all about the sex they had, right after he spanked her for doing it.

Sigh. To have someone who cared that much about whether or not your door was locked in a perfectly safe neighborhood, not to mention the adorably nosy neighbor Reid had who was as overprotective as Owen, was a dream.

Not to mention the spankings or whatever the hell else kink loving things I only dreamed about when I took that damn test existed out in the world.

Once again, the painful and hilarious reminder of my solo sex by battery charger life flashed before me. The smile that spread across my face, however, made my cheeks hurt because Reid deserved all the spankings she wanted after the shitty boyfriends she'd had to go through to find Owen and her HEA.

"Yoda lady-"

"Stop yodeling!" Reid yelled back from the kitchen as I shut the door behind me with a grin.

Two weeks ago, my masked friend sent me a video of two people in the back of the car, telling what had to be the worst knock-knock joke in history, and like any perfectly wonderful bestie, after I stopped crying from laughing because it was so bad, I promptly told it to Reid right before three customers came bustling through the door of Magpie.

She also was reduced to tears and mouthed *I hate you*, before helping the women pick out a few items while I cackled to myself and checked on a few leads for new pieces for the boutique.

Now it was our greeting whenever I swept in through the front door.

Okay, so I'd only done it three times, but still. It cracked me up, and I'd like to think it gave me extra bestie brownie points.

"I come bearing wine," Reid announced as I stuck my umbrella lovingly in the silver metal bin she had next to the table in the entryway before I took one of the glasses she held with a grin. "The only reason I love that damn joke is because Owen rolled his eyes when he laughed after I told it to him."

"I'm sure you were naked and he was all compliant and post orgasmic blissed out and therefore didn't realize how horrible it was," I snared and wrinkled my nose before taking a sip. "Oh, sweet first drink of Drunk Book Club, how I desperately need you."

Reid raised her brows. "Rough day?"

"Colder than it looks outside. Not my smartest idea. Plus I foolishly thought my sweater would be warm enough, but nope." I popped the 'p' and slugged back the rest of the white in the glass.

She jerked her head towards the parlor room. Never let it be said the parlor room at Grandma Lena's house didn't get used for all the things she hoped it would. "Come on, the rest of the bottle and blankets await."

"Blanket! Wine!"

"And *spicy* Drunk Book Club." I stifled a groan, because I somehow hoped she'd forget all about Delena Bennett's book and move on to other things. Like another book not written by her sex-starved best friend who kept the fact she was said writer from her.

The guilt ate away at my soul, so I poured another glass and downed it before she noticed. Then innocently filled it again like it was the first time when she turned and pointed at me with her glass.

"And now it's time to spill, Jessa Elizabeth." Her eyes narrowed, and I did my best to blink back as innocently as possible. "You made me take that damn test, tell you all about Owen and," her free hand flailed, "stuff-"

"Like how he likes it when you call him Daddy even though you won't," I teased, still trying for the distraction technique I thought I'd long ago mastered.

"Nice diversion, but you're not getting off the hook so easily."

A sigh escaped me before I could stop it, and I snatched my favorite fluffy blanket from the back of the couch before sitting with it over me so I could shake off the lingering chill. Stupid North Carolina rain. "Ain't that the truth."

"Jessa!"

"Reid! This is fun. Let's keep it going and that way you won't have to hear the boring details of my non-existent sex life which is bleeding frustration into every corner of my life so bad that I repainted my kitchen a few nights ago, ordered way too much Australian licorice, and can't concentrate on anything else but having an *actual* orgasm with someone else at least watching me get off."

The room fell silent as her eyes grew wide. Then she cleared her throat. "Well, does this mean we're adding exhibitionism to our kink list?"

Shit, was I?

"Jessa! Do you want some guy to watch you get off?"

My mouth opened to speak, but I couldn't get the words out. Or any words for that matter. So I did the next best thing as my cheeks reddened.

Because one night not too long ago I had been in my room, letting my favorite tingly buddy do its thing when I thought I saw something outside my window. Which was ridiculous, because the tall ass trees that hid my bedroom from the street or prying neighborly eyes made anyone sneaking a peek nearly impossible. And my neighbor, Matt, wasn't exactly interested in me. Or anyone with boobs.

But I couldn't shake the idea that someone was watching me.

And I really liked the idea.

"Hallelujah, I *finally* found a kink that makes you stop and think, which means YOU SO DO!" she squealed. A satisfied grin spread across her face as she leaned back in her favorite chair. Her jaw dropped, and she sat forward. "Wait, do you already have someone in mind? Jessa Elizabeth, I swear, I will withhold wine. And no more purses!"

I gasped. "You wouldn't!"

"Spill. You owe me after the first Drunk Book Club."

"Hey, that night led you to your HEA, kinky sex, that necklace," I cackled when her hand flew to the link, "which I *know* the meaning of, of my not so innocent bestie, kinky sex-"

"You already said that!"

"-and coffee in bed alongside whatever else. And, oh yeah, someone to spank you whenever you want!"

We glared at each other. Lips twitching until dissolving into giggles. When we finally regained our breath, I gave her the side eye. "Can we worry about this *after* Drunk Book Club?"

She shook her head. "Not happening because I know how

Drunk Book Club ends. Or sometimes ends. Owen is out of town until tomorrow night, and you can sleep over," she wheedled.

I opened my mouth, then shut it. Because a part of me wasn't sure *what* I wanted to do later tonight. When it got really dark.

Damn devil and angel were whispering all kinds of plans and ideas to my inner whore. Of course, she liked every damn idea flashing like lady porn over and over in my, er, her head.

Especially the one where he watched from outside. Wearing a mask. The image of the Fury game we watched from Maddie and Sebastian's place hit me. The players were all wearing those gator type things pulled up over their mouths on the sidelines, and Maddie and I had joked that they were book boyfriend material as Sebastian and Ty were shown on the screen.

Well, fuck. I glanced over at my purse on the couch next to me. The phone inside whispered to me to sneak into the bathroom and send a message to my…

Wait, what the fuck was I doing?

Way too much wine, and not enough carbs, I decided. Yep, that was it. The wine was enhancing my horniness and fantasies and making me reckless and all kinds of unspeakably dirty, filthy-

I blinked. Reid waved her hand in front of me again. "Now I know you're keeping something from me! You're never this quiet!"

"I'm so not quiet!"

The stare off lasted less than a second, before I gave in. "Fine. I'm maybe talking to someone, but it's not what you think. At all. And it's…complicated. Like, really complicated."

The doorbell rang, and Reid sighed as she stood. "Complicated how? Quick, so I can answer the damn door and I lose the chance to repay you for-"

"Spankings? Kinky sex? Praise and daddy kink?"

"Oh my God, Jessa!" she stood and spun on her heel to go answer the door. "You're not getting away with this!"

My chuckle died as I quickly pulled out my phone.

> Jessa: Ideally, if I had research opportunities available, my fellow researcher would be available when the opportunity arose. Correct?

Maddie's voice carried in from the hall, and the smell of Italian drifted down the hallway as they headed toward the kitchen. The couch nearly vibrated as my knee bounced up and down as I silently prayed for him to answer as quickly as he possibly could. I would never live it down if the girls found out I was not only writing romance, but asking a complete stranger to do what I was about to ask him. Online.

Or in person. Shit. My hand trembled, fidgeting while I threw a furtive glance at the door, hoping Maddie had some crazy future sister-in-law secret handshake or whatever to share before they came back and caught me.

> I'm all yours, Wildfire. Tell me what you need and I'll do it.

> Jessa: Anything?

> Anything.

My fingers never flew so fast, and when I was done, I hit send then held my breath. Waiting for his to response, and when it came, I almost did, too.

> I'll be there.

# CHAPTER 7

## TY

My hand twitched, and for the first time in my life, the idea of spanking someone made my cock come to life.

Full on, LFG action.

Jessa walked all the way to Sebastian's brother's place, which wouldn't have been a big deal, but fuck, there was a chill in the air on top of the rain. And she left her jacket at home. She hesitated a few houses down from her place, and glanced back home like she might turn around and go back to grab it but she didn't. And that's when it hit me.

The image of her bent over my lap, ass red from me reminding her to never do that again. Squirming against my cock, hard and jutting into her belly as she whimpered and defied me.

Yep, if there was one thing I knew about my Wildfire, it was that she was a full-on brat.

The glare when she snatched her Pom Guac from me? Not the first time my suspicions were confirmed.

And fuck if her attitude didn't make me want to make her

mine even more. Her fire, her spirit? The way she chased her dream, all by herself?

God, the woman was a goddess. A pain in the ass, to be sure. Sassy. And hiding a soul that probably made up stories when she was younger because she moved around so much. No siblings. No one to play with. At least I had cousins and an older brother for a while before he moved far away. No wonder she started writing in secret.

She'd been doing it her whole life.

Fucking rain. I didn't care that she loved walking in it, and chose to walk to Reid and Owen's place instead of driving because of it. I fought the urge to run up and give her my hoodie, consequences be damned.

Close enough to make sure she was ok but far enough away to make sure she didn't see me, I followed her until she walked up the steps and went inside. The tension in my body melted away, if only for a little while. She was safe inside, no doubt catching up with QB's future sister-in-law.

Having wine. And hopefully staying where she was tonight, even if it meant I'd miss seeing her crawl into bed, her ereader close by in case she couldn't sleep. Her body curled around her pillows until finally, her eyes closed, and her lips parted as she fell asleep.

Fuck. Me.

I waited outside, my SUV parked a few houses down from Reid's, where I left it a few hours ago after practice. The Wild Card game had everyone on edge, good and bad, and I'd had energy I ran off before I made my way to her house. The lights filtered through her curtains as she changed after work, and it took everything in me to not message her just to see the way her face changed when she read it.

But, I didn't want to push her. She had to make the decision. Not me. As much as I wanted to fulfill her fantasies, there was no way in hell I'd push her until she gave the go ahead.

My mind drifted, running over my checklist for my pre-game routine. Each detail planned, prepped, and ready to go. Then I did a run down of the things I'd added. Making sure Jessa's windows were secure, her backdoor locked. The cameras at Magpie monitored, both inside and out, for any trouble. Fuck, I even had her damn doorbell surveillance on my phone. Not to mention the camera I set up to make sure she was okay when I couldn't watch her.

I flicked my thumb, bringing up the screen with her name at the top. Fuck, she was the only name. Anonymous account, and there was no else I chatted with.

QB and I had our text chat going.

I grinned, sending him a message.

> If you're missing your girl, I can drop by.

Fully knowing he planned on stopping by and picking her up to take advantage of Drunk Book Club.

Where the book in question was written by none other than Delena Bennett herself. If only the girls knew the book they were all gushing over was penned by my Wildfire.

They'd freak out and be louder than the fan zone at the stadium when we secured our Wild Card berth. Cause my girl?

She wrote some fucking hot shit. With actual plot.

And that damn chapter with the fucking ties?

No doubt whatever she needed 'research help' with would make my cock the happiest fucker on the planet.

> QB: I know you miss me more, but you'll just have to wait. Ember gets all hot and bothered after DBC and there's no fucking way I'm giving that up. Even for your ass.

Aw, you like my ass.

> QB: You're such an ass. Rest up.

Love you, too.

> QB: middle finger emoji followed by a heart

Dude loved me. I grinned in the dark, feeling pretty fucking good.

The ping on my phone notifications pulled my thoughts out of the mental evaluation and bromance moment.

> Jessa: Ideally, if I had research opportunities available, my fellow researcher would be available when the opportunity arose. Correct?.

I'm all yours, Wildfire. Tell me what you need, and I'll do it.

> Jessa: Anything?

Anything.

I held my breath as the dots danced on the screen.

> Jessa: I want you to watch me from outside my window and text me what to do. With a mask on.

*Well, fuck me, Wildfire.* Sitting became the most uncomfortable thing I'd ever done in my life my dick was so hard.

I'll be there.

## CHAPTER 8

### JESSA

"And then Owen read it out loud, that damn smirk on his face while he told me to loosen the damn tie he wore. I swear, I turned into Niagara Falls," Reid hissed while her big sister, Kylie, and Alex went to grab a few waters from the fridge.

Two hours into DBC, and my cheeks were so fucking flushed, not from the wine, but from hearing everyone rant and rave about Britt and Noah, the FMC and MMC in my book, Don't Walk Away.

Hearing how much the girls loved the story, the smexy times (their words and not mine) had me filled with the kind of warm fuzzies I'd only dreamed about. Reviews were for readers and I steadfastly avoided them at all cost. But, here and now, the girls were impossible to ignore.

The guilt over keeping my pen name a secret hit me about twenty minutes in. Trapped between preening and feeling like the biggest fake in the world, I nursed my wine, making excuses to sneak away to check my phone far from prying eyes.

Only Kylie caught me sneaking away with a weird expression on her face, but I quickly ran to the bathroom.

To reread the messages, throw my hands over my face, and ignore the fact that I was ready to leave the minute the rest of the girls arrived.

Not because of them or DBC. But because I was horny as fuck and done with solo orgasms. Even if it was only with someone watching, if I didn't get off soon, I was liable to commit a crime and blame it on my inner whore.

And the devil and angel on my shoulders.

Earning me a few weeks stay in a padded room, where no joint orgasms would be remotely possible.

Sucking in deep breath, I clasped the door knob, twisted it, and headed back out into the battle. Determined to make my escape to Project Commanded Masked Orgasm Research.

"Hey, Jessa, I think your Uber is outside." Reid called from the couch. Everyone else sat around the parlor room in smaller pairs, picking out their favorite scenes. Color my cheek red as fuck.

My brows drew together. "I didn't-"

> The car is there. No walking home in the rain.
> Research starts now, Wildfire. DM when
> you're in your bedroom.

Well, fuck me sideways and pull my hair until I scream your name. Shit. Now I was using Ty's sayings. Fuck me sideways, indeed.

I smirked, so turned on my fingers barely functioned.

> Jessa: Is this where I say, "Yes, sir"?

Dots jumped.

> Only if you don't want to face the consequences. And it's Sir, Wildfire.

Color my panties useless. I was suddenly very happy with the chunky sweater I threw on over my leggings. Darn nipples would definitely give something away because the room was toasty and cozy like Christmas morning. That could be because the Holly Jolly sat like it was too damn proud to be put away for the year around Reid's house.

"Anything interesting?" Kylie asked.

"Shit, you scared me!"

She chuckled. "Sorry. I just never see you flustered, Jessa." Also said this while not appearing in the least bit sorry. More like amused as fuck as my flusteryness.

"Didn't sleep well last night." I smiled, my excuse weak and we both knew it. With a wave to the room, I called, "I am out, DBCers. Don't read and not enjoy it, if you know what I mean. See you later, Reid! Have fun later with your pun-"

"Just go! Oh my God!"

I chuckled as I bolted for the door, but every nerve in my body lit with a fire that needed something only my masked stranger could give me.

*Bring it on, Masked Man,* the trio of evil, horny doers in my head whispered gleefully. I might've joined in, too.

# CHAPTER 9

## TY

> Jessa: Your mission, should you choose to fulfill a writer's research fantasy mission. Tell me you want to watch me come, and you're in charge of everything I do. From outside my window wearing a mask.

*J*essa stepped out the door, her feet made quick work of the front stoop stairs leading to the sidewalk. Her eyes darted both ways before she opened the door of the car I ordered for her. The driver, Eddie, was a regular for the team, and used to picking up the other players' girlfriends or wives for the guys. But she didn't know that. And he thought she was just a friend that needed a ride home but hated asking anyone for favors.

Not too far from the truth. But, he also played up the Uber driver facade due to the extra hundred I promised him.

To save her embarrassment.

In reality, it was to keep my identity secret. They exchanged the usual info to secure the ride, then he pulled from the curb and drove in the direction of Jessa's house. I followed far enough behind that I could see her but she wouldn't notice my black SUV.

My eyes darted to my phone sitting in the mount on the dash. The red dot blinked as Eddie turned the corner up ahead.

There was no way in hell I trusted anyone with her, even though all the guys vouched for Eddie. I knew where Jessa was at all times thanks to the tracker I remote installed. Sometimes having a friend who knew more about the ins and outs of cybersecurity than you did had its perks. And now I owed Dante a favor. Or favors.

The dot slowed a few minutes later as the driver pulled in front of her house. Jessa tried to give him a tip before he left, but Eddie waved her off. He waited until she entered the house, then pulled away.

A few houses down along where the street curved there was a tree that partially blocked my SUV from Jessa's place. The rain finally stopped just before she left Reid's townhouse. The streets gleamed and the air held just enough humidity to make the chill in the air noticeable for this time of year.

I pulled up the gaiter mask around my neck, my hood already in place as I made my way closer to Jessa's. After making sure the street was empty, I typed out a message.

> Bad girl. Already not following my directions.

One side of mouth quirked up, already seeing the indignation in her expression in my head when she read that one. The dots danced as she typed her response.

> Jessa: I just walked in the door, Sir.

> Two minutes ago, Wildfire. Tsk tsk.

Insert patented Jessa eye-roll and the huff she did when she felt she was right. I'd witnessed it a few times when we were all out together. Fuck, I loved her attitude. My cock twitched, wanting her. Needed her defiance and craved the way she talked back, so sure and trusting of me without knowing who I was. At least on the outside.

> Jessa: It's not like you can spank me right now. I can be as bad as I want.

Oh, if she only knew how much fun I could have making her wish she could have a spanking instead of what I had planned for her.

All the roads, lost loves, ups and downs, all led to this moment. To her. To the one person who fit into my heart, the places I unknowingly saved for her.

Jessa might think no one saw her the way she craved to be seen, but I did. Her spirit, all the moments of bravado. The fierce way she watched after the people she cared about, all the while holding back so she wouldn't be hurt. Her heart safe behind walls she erected no one could tear down until me.

> Don't be so sure that the only punishment you'll earn is a spanking.

> Bedroom. Go to the window.

Lights clicked on, then off, as she moved from room to room. Living room, kitchen, hallway, and finally, her bedroom. The trees rustled with the breeze as I stood back from her window. Watching. Waiting.

She caught my eye. Ever since the first time I laid eyes on her. Every damn move she made, in the light or the dark.

Even from the sidelines, I knew one thing in the second it took for fucking lightning to strike.

And now, I watched her from the shadows, knowing someday soon, she would be mine.

The light next to her bed clicked on, filling the room with a soft glow. Her body took step after step to the window, her movements jerked with nervous energy. Her chin held high, eyes searching until I took one step forward, still shrouded in shadow from the street lights. Eyes locked with mine. A gasp escaped her lips as the reality of what we were doing hit her. But she didn't back away, or close the curtains.

A shaky hand came up and opened the curtains further. Behind her, her bed loomed. My cock hardened, imagining holding her down, driving into her as her whimpers and moans filled the room. Fuck.

*Focus, Ty. Get her off. Fantasy to reality. Make her realize how fucking much she needs this. Us.*

> Take everything off. Leave on your bra and panty.

Her breath hitched as she read the message, lips parting. When her gray eyes met mine again, darkened with desire and filled with all the things we both needed my hand clenched. The need to touch her skin, painful. A solitary moment passed between us, then she slowly began to remove every shred of clothing until she stood in only her purple lace bra and panty.

Not breaking contact, she backed up until she hit the foot of her bed, covers and pillows all in place, phone still in hand. When she reached the middle, I sent her another message.

> Toy. The purple one.

God I loved how she responded. Eyes flashing but obeying every damn command I gave her, taking the toy out of the drawer of the nightstand.

> That's my fucking good girl. Show me how you get off with it, but don't come until I say you can. Put the phone next to you. I'll send another one when I want you to stop. Nod if you understand.

When I looked up, she nodded, biting her bottom lip, and pulled her panties to the side. Her pretty pink pussy on display just for me. And when she turned on the toy, rubbing along her clit, I nearly came in my fucking pants.

Jessa was going to be my undoing. But before I made her fantasy come true, she fell apart just for me.

## CHAPTER 10

### JESSA

My body tensed, already on the edge. All the pent up tension and desperate need for... something ready to crash over me. The sweet relief of whatever this was, building and threatening to explode before I had a chance to catch my breath. But I stopped.

Because he watched me from just a few feet away.

*I couldn't come until he told me to*, I reminded myself. The freedom of someone else controlling the thing I thought about, wanted, hell, *needed* more than I realized until this very moment chased away any doubts.

Any embarrassment over being open to his gaze, the most intimate part of me there for him to see. I slid the purple toy along my clit, gasping when it brushed the sensitive bundle of nerves. Panting like a damn cat in heat. Inner whore, meet horny and slutty Jessa.

The devil and angel high fived, loving how close the precipice was, how this slow torture sent small shockwaves along my spine. My pussy throbbing as I slid the slickened vibrator in, slowly. Back nearly bowing off the bed from the sensation. When I opened my eyes to see him standing at the window, I whimpered. He shuddered like he heard me.

The phone buzzed at my left. I looked over.

> Use your fingers. No coming yet. Spread yourself for me.

How easily I complied, opening my thighs.

> Good little whore, aren't you?

Shit. Did the man find my damn kink test results? Praise me, then degrade me. Punish me, and make me come. Or don't. Edge me until I begged to come.

I couldn't form a coherent thought as my fingers slid along my clit, the wetness an obvious sign that my impending orgasm wouldn't take much more than a few more moments. But I held on, knowing he hadn't told me when I could let go and finally shatter and fall apart. The sounds I made, desperate and full of need. My body begging and pleading for release.

He stood, watching, only his eyes visible. The mask, so like the ones I pictured earlier, covering his features. Even so, I felt safe even as the thrill of the scene made me make a sound of frustration. My eyes followed the movement of his arm, realizing his hand was not visible.

Fuck, was he getting off, watching me touch myself.

The thought almost tipped me over the edge, but he shook his head in warning. My phone lit up.

> Not yet. You were a bad girl. No coming until I tell you. Up on your knees. Bra off. Fuck my pussy with the toy like you'd ride me. Don't look away from me or you can't come tonight.

I scrambled up to my knees, one hand undoing the clasp at my back. My nipples jutted out and I skimmed my hands down the front of my body. Enough to tease him, brushing the hardened points as his eyes narrowed in warning. I pinched one, gasping at the sensation, wishing it was his hand. With my other hand, I reached for the toy, still vibrating and slid it easily into my pussy. I let out a strangled yelp, my hips moving as I imagined it was his cock buried inside.

He watched, arm moving and flexing as he stroked himself. I growled, wishing I could see, but I didn't dare look away.

I needed to come so badly that I was ready to defy him and damn the consequences. Just as I was about to, he nodded, and my world exploded around me. My body trembled and shook as wave after wave of pleasure crashed over me, relentless and intense.

When I could finally move again as the world stopped spinning, I sat up on my elbows. But he was gone, the space he controlled my body from, empty. Like he'd never been there.

The light filtered in from the moon, reminding me how alone I was as I pursed my lips, saddened by his absence after having the best orgasm quite possibly of my life. Then noticed the final message he'd sent minutes ago.

> I left you a few things by your front door.
> Lock up after, Wildfire. Sweet dreams.

A soft breeze drifted passed me into the house when I opened the door, curiosity overriding my post-orgasm bliss need for sleep.

The nondescript brown paper bag sat there, lonely and obviously needing a friend, so like any kind human being with an overwhelming need to know what the fuck was inside, I picked it up.

Inside was a bottle of the same dragon fruit juice I loved in my margs, still cold, a container of Pom Guac, a bag of Darrell Lea licorice, a eucalyptus bath bomb, and a handwritten note that read…

*You're fucking gorgeous when you fall apart for me, Wildfire. That's my fucking girl. I'm so proud of you. Go write that scene. It's everything.*

# CHAPTER 11

## TY

"Sweet Jesus, QB, you look like you need this more than me," I joked as I nudged Sebastian with my shoulder as we boarded the plane to New Orleans. The Wild Card game berth came as no surprise to the organization, but the rest of the football world acted like the secrets of Area 51 were revealed when we won the game that got us on this flight.

I handed him the coffee in my right hand as we climbed the stairs to the team plane, and he grunted his thanks. The scene from last night played on constant repeat in my head, and fuck, I only hoped it would pause when football needed my attention.

I fucking doubted it though. The vision of Jessa coming hit all the highlight reel qualifications, and my cock loved every damn replay.

"Simmons, if the world didn't already think we were in some sort of relationship-"

"Bromance, QB."

"-I'd fucking hug you right now. Maddie was all riled up after 'Drunk Book Club' and damned if I was going to let that go to waste," he grumbled, taking a sip as he sat in the leather seat.

The new owners decided that we deserved the first-class treatment this trip. Not that we had a ghost story biplane for the other away games, but this plane was next level. I half-expected to wake up and find myself in the team plane we usually flew in.

Most of the organization was on one of two chartered flights heading to New Orleans, and the team even arranged for most of the team's families to make the game if they wanted, on commercial flights, over the next few days.

Monday night games meant prime time TV. Prime time meant more exposure. And being the underdogs this season meant we were under a microscope. The pressure, while intense, also made us hungrier than our competition. QB and the offensive line had a bet going with the D on who was going to make the plays.

My bet?

The motherfucking Fury. We all won, or not at all.

But still, I couldn't wait to see who was going to host the end of the year barbecue. Losing line had to talk Frankie into catering the entire thing. And Frankie never did anything outside the Prickly Pear without making sure it was well worth his while.

"Simmons, are you going to settle and let the wind keep you steady, or stand in the face of obscurity making us late?" Xavier asked as he pushed past me with a grin.

I chuckled and sat down next to Sebastian, who was scrolling through his phone.

"How the hell do you understand him?" he grumbled, a smirk on his face.

"Easy. Laid back. Plus I spent a year living in Hawaii with my cousins. One year of surfing the waves and you can interpret anything. Zen. Or whatever." I nodded to his phone. "Mads?"

He grinned. "She sent me a few pictures last night before I picked her up from Owen's. Those girls had way too fun with that damn book. Whoever this Delena whatever her name is, I owe her."

"Bennett."

"What?"

"Last name is Bennett. Well, pen name, anyway."

"How do you know this shit?"

I shrugged, careful not to say too much that might give Jessa, or me, away. "I eat and I know things," I joked, popping a chip in my mouth from the trays the flight attendants passed out as we boarded.

Sebastian shook his head. "Just make sure you don't start reading those books and expecting it to be real life."

I smirked. "What? I'm not book boyfriend material, QB."

"Simmons, not many of us are."

Little did he know Delena's next book boyfriend was closer than he thought.

---

*Game day.*

Nerves steady, and every item on my prep list checked off. Even so, I ran down my checklist again.

And the best thing I double checked? Jessa.

I worried she'd wake up the morning after filled with regret. Or worse, she'd block me. Ignore my good morning.

But she didn't. As soon as I sent it to her, she responded.

> Good morning, Wildfire.

> Jessa: Good morning, Mr. Incredible.

Pixar reference?

> Jessa: Thor?

Big hammer. I like it.

> Jessa: Dr. Strange?

Hmmm.

> Jessa: Are you an X-Men guy? Can't see you going DC.

Gambit.

> Jessa: That I can see. Card tricks?

No. He knows what he wants, and does what he has to to get it.

She didn't answer right away, the dots missing. Worried I went too far, I almost sent an apology, but then…

> Jessa: Did you get what you want then?

Not even close, Wildfire. I want it all.

> Jessa: I'm not sure I can give you that. Yet.

No rush, baby. I'm a patient man. I know when something's worth the wait.

# CHAPTER 12

## JESSA

"I can't watch," Maddie moaned, eyes covered by both of her hands as she bounced up and down on her toes. Her eyes peeked out between her fingers and she gasped.

Halftime loomed, just minutes away, which really meant more than just a few minutes, because everyone knew no football game ever lasted as long as the play clock did. The first half, which said 30 minutes of play time, currently hit 86 minutes on my watch.

Thank God the suite we were in had food. And drinks. Because if I had to sit through this and not eat my nervous feelings, I might turn carnivorous. The Fury were only down by a field goal, which was so much less than the odds makers had them at for the game against New Orleans.

"Thirty-seconds left," Reid murmured. Behind us, Owen peered over his shoulder like one of those sexy body guards looming over his client.

Ooooh! Book boyfriend idea. I might not write about my friends' sex lives, because my overly active not getting any imagination took care of that, but it didn't mean inspiration didn't hit me all the time from just being around.

And who didn't like a forbidden relationship? Especially if the FMC made the hot, sexy Marine Vet bodyguard's life insane and his cock really ready to teach her a lesson or three?

Except, did the masked mutual touch and order sitch mean I was no longer getting any?

Because inner whore and her two buddies were screaming for me to beg for more research time.

"Which means at least three minutes," I quipped, tipping my red Solo cup to the field where, "Football time is even worse than book girl math."

"So much worse than girl math," Reid agreed, and yelped when Owen smacked her on the ass then kissed the top of her head from behind.

"Girl math?"

I shot him a look over my shoulder, adding my best death-by-chocolate glare. Can't help it, I really want one of those damn muffins from home. "First, the two of you are making me and my inner whore jealous-"

"Jessa!" Reid shrieked, cheeks flushed with embarrassment, which only earned her another smack for Owen who just shrugged after and motioned for me to continue.

"And girl math makes any problem, purchase, or idea work because we want it to."

"Will girl math make Ty connect when Sebastian throws on the next play?" Maddie asked.

Surprisingly, the Fury fans followed down to the Crescent City, and the noise level was beyond deafening.

"I mean, anything's possible." I shrugged and took a sip. Sebastian and Ty's Bromance made their on-field chemistry one of the reasons the team garnered so much momentum after the game where they lost the second string kicker and had to do two-point conversions the entire game. Which started the fairy tale season upswing.

"Sebastian said Ty's focus has been next level." Owen nodded at the empty cup in Reid's hand. "Be right back, Angel." He made his way down the short aisle of seats, as my other bestie smiled the way only a girl living her best life could.

"So, then by all accounts, they should totally connect." Maddie nodded.

The teams lined up for the last play of the half, with only seconds left on the clock.

Third and ten.

Sebastian called out a play, probably something like 'Taylor 22 Evermore Exhausting Kittens Wine Tangerine" or some nonsense.

Ty took off from his spot on the end, splitting behind the line of scrimmage, blocked on a defensive player, then slipped up the center and down the field. The world moved in slow motion as Sebastian twisted, fake pumped, then hurled the football down the field like it was a shooting star, straight into Ty's hands. He moved to the left, avoiding one defensive player, then the other, and shot down the field straight into the end zone.

*TOUCHDOWN FURY!*

Ty pumped his arm in the air as Sebastian ran down the field and jumped onto the tight end as the crowd went crazy. He backed up and flashed the number two at the line.

"Wait, I didn't know Tall, Dark, and Not Asshole was a Swifty!"

"Two-point conversion, not 22, J." Reid snorted. The entire suite erupted as, once again, Sebastian and Ty connected. "I don't know if I can handle another half of this."

"Oh, I make him listen. Especially in the middle of the night in the kitchen. While he makes me a midnight snack."

"Midnights album?" I asked, and Maddie raised her hand for a high five.

"Hell yes."

"Oh my God," Reid moaned.

"Which is why we need another drink and food, then we can suffer through another thirty minutes that somehow warps into an impossibly longer and stress-ridden display of male aggression."

"Sounds like sex to me," Miranda, the lawyer for the Fury joked as she came up beside me. "Without the stress, of course."

"Ah, but sometimes stress *is* involved. The pressure to make a decision if things aren't working, or if you're just too overwhelmed by the rest of your life to have to figure out if he wants his dick su-"

"Jessa!" Reid threw her hands over her ears as tears rolled down her cheeks she was laughing so hard.

I shrugged, not in the least bit sorry. Miranda was doing her best not to laugh but losing the battle. "I like you."

I curtsied. "Thank you. Ditto."

The icy blonde flipped her hair over her shoulder and nodded at someone on the other side of the room. "And I think you should find someone to make sex less stressful. After the game, maybe?"

"That's no fun. If they were amazing and only in NOLA then every other encounter of my life would pale in comparison." As if they all didn't already after a night night with Mr. Stalkery-Masked-Command-Me-To-Come hadn't already.

"Truth. Either way, Res wanted me to make sure your accommodations were ok for the evening, and wanted to remind you if you needed anything to let him or Kellan know. I have a few more hands to shake, and a sponsorship deal to get signed, but it was lovely," she winked, "to see you all again." She wiggled her fingers and went off to wherever it was these things happened.

"We really need to expand Drunk Book Club. Too bad Delena Bennett's next book doesn't come out for another two months."

Ha. If only they knew. Because until my not so solo performance the other night, I had considered moving the release of my next book two more months ahead. If I published it at all.

Owen groaned. "Any more members and you'll need a security detail to keep an eye on you."

"Aw, baby. You know you love the post-meeting per-"

"Room. Hallway. Something. Get one." I pretended to cover my ears, but couldn't hide the smile on my face as Reid planted a big kiss on Owen's mouth, and Maddie high fived me. "Drunk Book Club is the best foreplay ever. Even when you have a solo performance."

Reid smacked me playfully on the arm. "Refills. Food. Now. Before the only clock that actually tells real time is up and it's third quarter time."

I hung back just enough so that I could check my phone.

> Hope you're loving the game, Wildfire. I can't stop thinking about the way you look when you come for me.

My poor panties had no chance.

Inner whore, Devil, and Angel had a quick conference and decided on a referendum. Which passed unanimously.

> Jessa: Maybe next time you can be in the same room, and find out how I feel when I do.

And then I realized I never told him or posted on my author account where I was or what I was doing.

"My hand might fall off," Reid muttered.

The entire stadium vibrated with the same nervous energy filled the suite.

Two minute warning.

The odds makers had never been so wrong. In fact, I'd bet a few of them were looking around wondering what the actual fuck was happening, because a team they had counted out because of a 'rebuilding' year was going to beat the team that only missed a play off clinched spot because of injuries in their last two games was on the cusp of being beat by the underdog.

Seconds ticked by, and that two point conversion was everything right now. The defense kept the other team from scoring on their last possession.

The Fury were down by two points. All we needed was a field goal. Twenty more yards and we would hit the longest distance our kicker ever made one by.

Running down the clock the last two plays, and now, with only twenty-seconds on the play clock, Sebastian took the snap, of course to another ridiculous play call in my head, this time, he handed off to Ty, who spun out of a defender's grasp, only to shoot the ball like a bullet to the rookie wide receiver, Mason Bryant, who ran it past the needed yardage, and within field goal distance.

The suite, and the entire stadium, erupted in cheers and disbelief from the home team fans as the special teams unit took the field. On the sideline, Ty and Sebastian watched, along with everyone else as our kicker raised his hand, and ran forward as the ball snapped into place.

When the ref raised his hands to confirm the field goal, Reid, Maggie and I screamed and forced Owen into our hug, jumping and screaming.

Fury ahead by one as the play clock hit zero.

On the field, the team streamed out, congratulating each other. The celebration filled the air in the stadium with electric energy that was contagious. I spun with a grin and watched as Sebastian and Ty high fived. My eyes narrowed as Ty stood back, and nodded at his best friend.

For some reason, heat pooled in my core watching him. Like there was something in the back of my mind pushing and telling me something I wasn't ready to acknowledge yet.

But all I could think about was getting home to my masked admirer.

# CHAPTER 13

## TY

"And that is how the cake has the fireworks and yellow brick road."

The buses waited to take us from the airport to the training center, and as we loaded on, Sebastian leaned over and muttered, "Translate."

I smirked, "Xav means that's how it's done." On the outside, I celebrated with my teammates, because hell yes, we won the game no one thought we had a chance in hell of winning.

But on the inside? I itched to get to Jessa. See her, because she flew home with the rest of the girls a few hours earlier. After that last message she sent, my cock went into overtime.

Fuck that. More like a driving *need* to get to her, even though I knew exactly where she was. At home.

Waiting for me.

~

Last chance, Wildfire. Once I'm inside, there's no going back.

The streetlights in front of Jessa's place cast shadows from the trees on the front porch as I waited in the darkness for her response. I shifted, adjusting myself because I'd never wanted anyone as much as I wanted her. Her smile, the way she challenged me even when she didn't realize it, and fuck, how she sank so far into my being that I'd never be able to let her go?

Mine.

From the first time she walked past the window at Magpie to when her smile lit up my fucking soul and stole my heart. Became my obsession.

> Jessa: No going back.

A second later, I pulled up the gaiter, covering my face before climbing up the steps to her door.

*Snick.* Air whooshed out of my lungs, my body on fire as I entered. Ready to find my fucking good girl and ruin her for anyone else. From this night on, the only man she'd ever want inside her body, heart, and soul would be me.

The door clicked closed as I stepped inside. I paused and peered into the darkness as my eyes adjusted. A soft hum from the refrigerator broke the silence as the ice maker turned on. A light over the sink that overlooked her back yard softly lit the way to her bedroom. If I hadn't been in here to leave her a few of her favorite things over the past few weeks, the light would've helped me find my way to her bedroom.

But, I knew exactly where she waited, even in the dark. Saw her in my mind's eye, laid out on the white and gray comforter on her bed. Pillows tossed carelessly on the floor, like she did every night before going to bed.

How many steps it took to get to her room. The switch that turned on the hall light. Bathroom door, guest room.

Then hers.

My feet fell soundlessly as I neared the bedroom door, my breath heavy underneath the mask as I pictured her, over and over. Knowing that after tonight, neither of us would ever be the same.

Just outside the door, I peered in through the small crack. The door sat ajar, the opening just enough that I caught sight of her silhouette in the darkness. A glow from her phone lit her face as she stared at it. Waiting. Lips parted, eyes wide. Chest rising and falling as her breathing quickened. Clad only in a pair of lace boyshorts and a matching bra, hair up in a messy bun that girls do. Neck exposed. Her body silently begged for my touch as she shifted, restless.

As turned as I was. I spotted a black scarf hanging from the mirror in front of her. With a smirk no one had a chance of seeing beneath the mask I wore, I typed and hit send before sticking my phone in my back pocket.

> Grab the scarf on the mirror. Then go sit on the edge of the bed like the good fucking girl you are.

Enraptured, my eyes followed her movements as she slowly took a few steps forward. Her eyes darted around the room, eyes narrowed.

*There's my little brat,* I thought. The thought of how I was going to show her how much I fucking loved her fire made my cock twitch in anticipation. If only Jessa understood how sexy I found it that she made me work for her, pushing limits and not giving in until I reminded her. A small creak of the door, and her head shot up, hand grabbing the scarf as she backed up until she hit the edge of the bed and sat.

Eyes locked on the spot I stood in the darkness. With one hand on the hard surface of the door, I slowly pushed it open, the low creak deafening in the silence of her home.

Breath held as I waited, watching her as I gauged her reaction from the doorway. One arm on the doorframe, controlling the need to grab her and make her mine. Touch her body. Devour her, taste every fucking inch of her. Everywhere. Throw her back onto the bed, spread her legs, and bury my nose between her thighs, breathing in her scent.

Even without any light I could see her tits, ready to spill out, rising and falling as her breath quickened. A slender hand twisted in the scarf as it wrapped around her fingers, her other hand gripping the thin strip of silk fabric like a lifeline.

Her lips parted, like she wanted to say something, but she sat, silent. Eyes begging for things she couldn't, or wouldn't, voice out loud. The things good girls shouldn't want, according to society.

Things *my* fucking good girl deserved. But only from me.

With a low growl, I stalked towards her. A dark chuckle as she jutted out her breasts, eyes wide with a mixture of fear, desire, and arousal. Fuck, I could smell how much she wanted this. Wanted me.

Did she have any idea who I was? That I watched her in the light *and* the dark?

## CHAPTER 14

### JESSA

A nagging voice in the back of my mind kept trying to get my inner whore to tell me something, but the bitch was too focused on how happy my long-neglected lady parts were going to be. As in, an actual person would be joining me, and not just the battery operated, charge me baby one more time, toys that had been a staple in my not-love-life for the past however many I don't want to admit months.

No matter that the message wasn't really a warning, but more of, *bitch, fucking listen because you're missing a key element here* kinda vibe.

The morning after the Fury's win, on the plane ride home, I sat with my earbuds in, the seat next to me empty, which never happened, and happily typed away. Maddie and the rest of the group were a few rows ahead of me, still riding the high of a win no one saw coming.

Well, no one except Sebastian and Ty, both who were so excited when we went out to dinner after the game at some fancy place the Fury owners took the team and their families to, they didn't stop smiling the entire night.

And Owen hugging his brother when we finally found

him after the game, and then again at dinner, definitely sparked those reverse harem trope vibes in my head. But, only if they were step-brothers and *not* dating my besties.

But a girl could fantasize, right?

Only problem? The fantasy of RH quickly warped into not two seriously hot step-brothers, but a masked tall, dark, and cinnastalker who told my no longer *inner* whore what to do and called me his good fucking girl.

And suspiciously reminded me of someone, but I couldn't quite put my finger on who.

Just as the tingle started to spark into something, Ty Simmons brushed up against me. My body, already on high *please fuck me, sir,* alert went into overtime. Stakes high, take me now level up as he apologized. My eyes locked on his lips, his tongue as he wet them. Green eyes staring into mine like he wanted to say something, but just as he opened his mouth, Mason Bryant walked in. The noise level increased as the rookie blushed, cheers and congratulations tossed around like confetti. In the mayhem, Ty and I were separated and he was gone before I knew what was happening hit my senses faster than any tequila shot I'd ever done on an empty stomach and wiped out any further of Ty and whatever he was going to say.

> Name the time and place. There's nothing I fucking want more than to feel you come around my cock like the good little whore I know you are for me.

Oh, holy hell and then some. My pussy clenched, begging me to answer. Before I knew what the hell I was doing, the wicked trio (inner whore, devil, and angel) took over my body and responded before I could even stop myself.

*Sigh*. Not that there was a chance in ever-loving hell I'd stop them from hitting send. Because they were me, as much as I'd denied it. If anything, I'd be there, cheering them on while crawling and begging on my knees for *him* to use me in any way he wanted.

> Jessa: Tomorrow night. My place. Come inside.

Oh, Wildfire. Don't say things you don't mean.

I bit my lip as I glanced around the room, sure my face told everyone exactly the kind of things I meant. Every single dirty, mess me up and *make me yours* fantasy.

> Jessa: I never say anything I don't mean or want.

And what exactly do you want?

The noise and people in the room faded away, and for a moment I swore my body heated with the kind of desire only having someone watching you and knowing how much you want them could bring.

> Jessa: You. Taking me, using me. Making me yours. If only for a night.

One night would never be enough. But we'll start there.

And now, I stood in my bedroom, half naked. Pussy so wet, my inner thigh was dripping with my arousal.

Staring at the masked man who lived in my fantasies. A moment away from begging on my hands and knees for him to fuck me. I twisted the black silk scarf around my hands, the slick softness against my skin in contrast to how badly I needed something, anything, to happen before I screamed.

Green eyes stared back at me, daring me to defy him. But I couldn't, any more than I could run from the room to stop what was about to happen between us. My breath caught as he stepped into the room, larger than I imagined yet he moved with a grace only a man confident in himself and his actions did.

His hand reached out when he closed in on me, the heat from his body radiating off of him. Bathing me in the warmth, pooling low in my belly. My legs opened as he stepped even closer. Back arched as I desperately pushed myself closer, needing his hands on me. Contact, wanting and a frenzied need for him. He took the scarf from me, eyes boring into mine. The intensity of his gaze hotter than anything I imagined. The scent of his skin, the brief touch of hand against mine, became too much, and I let out a frustrated growl.

He chuckled as I glared at him. "Patience. Good girls get rewarded."

*Holy. Hell.*

"Turn around," he ordered, voice rough and low. "Now."

I scrambled to obey, kneeling on the bed before him. The instant his front touched my back, the feel of his hoodie, the zipper cool against my back, my head dropped back. A hand snaked around, making its way up my belly, between my breasts, leaving chills in its wake. When his hand encircled my neck, I gasped.

Voice a harsh whisper in my ear, he rasped, "Close your eyes."

The soft silk covered my eyes as I obeyed, and my senses came alive as he secured the scarf into place. I nearly jumped out of my skin with pleasure as his lips skimmed along the side of my neck, exposed, breath hot and heavy on my skin.

"Fuck, you taste even better than I imagined."

His growl shot to my pussy, hands skimming my shoulders then making his way between my shoulder blades. The heat from his skin burning me in the most delicious way possible. "Down. Ass in the air."

A gentle push, and my face was on the bed. I whimpered as he slid the lace boyshorts, soaked with my arousal, down past my thighs. His intake of breath sent shivers down my body as he repositioned me, spreading my legs so my pussy was exposed. Every intimate part of my body there for him to see. My cheeks flushed.

"Fuck, your panties are so fucking wet. Such a needy little brat, aren't you?"

I started to push myself up on my elbows but he made a disapproving sound before gently pushing me back down. A sharp smack on my ass followed. I yelped in protest.

He leaned down and licked the sensitive shell of my ear, and murmured, "I didn't say you could move, did I?" I shook my head. "Say it. I want to hear how needy you are with your ass in the air. Knowing I can see every fucking part of you."

It was then I realized he must've removed the mask covering the lower part of his face. Fuck, I wanted to see him. But another part of me was so fucking turned on and afraid to do break this heady feeling that I whispered, "No, you didn't."

"That's my good fucking girl," he purred, landing another sharp smack on my ass.

I stifled a moan as he unsnapped my bra from the back. When his tongue licked a path from the base of my spine, up, I nearly came just from the sensation alone. The loss of my sight only meant my other senses were heightened, and every touch, even his weight shifting on the bed, shot to my pussy.

"Your ass looks so damn pretty right now, wearing my handprint. Better than I've imagined," he murmured, voice low, sexy, and everything I'd dreamed. Familiar, but I pushed the thought away as his hand smoothed the heated skin.

*I'd never tease Reid about getting spanked ever again*, I thought as he delivered one more before spreading my open to his perusal.

His tongue licked a path from my ass to my clit, and I couldn't hold back the yell as he grazed his teeth on my clit. The tight bundle of nerves, already swollen from whatever the hell we had been doing, nearly exploded as he continued to lick and suck. Devouring me like a man starved and I was the only meal he could imagine having ever again in his life.

Over and over, he tasted and fucked my pussy with his tongue. Not letting me have a moment to breathe or shift position, hands keeping me open and at his pleasure. And there was no doubt, it was. The feral noises coming from him vibrated against my sensitive skin, and the wetness between my thighs and all over his face almost made me blush. Had I actually given a fuck at that moment.

But, my body tensed, and the orgasm I'd been holding back crashed through the gates I tried to lock. I didn't want him to stop, but I also needed to come so badly that as I finally did, I screamed, stars swimming before my eyes even though I was blindfolded.

Again and again, wave after wave exploded. He didn't stop, relentless in his pursuit.

Until I felt him pull back, his mouth suddenly gone. Terrified he left me, I tried to sit up, only to have him growl, "Now, I'm going to fuck your pussy so damn hard that you'll be ruined for any other man. *Ever. Mine.*"

In my blissed-out state, I barely heard the tearing of a condom wrapper. Seconds later, I felt him at my entrance before he slammed himself home, driving into my slickness with a fervor that shoved me up the bed.

One hand reached around, and he pinched my clit, sending spirals of pleasure along my body as another orgasm threatened. "This pussy is *mine. Say it.*"

"It's yours!" I screamed, coming again.

"That's my fucking good girl. Come all over my cock. Such a dirty little whore, you love my cock, don't you?"

*Oh shit,* I thought as I rode the tremors wracking my body, an endless series of pleasure that seemed to go on and on. His breathing became more harsh. A finger slid from the base of my spine, teasing the tight hole as his other hand spread me open.

"Fuck, every single hole is mine. I can't wait to fuck you here. Take your ass while you squirm, begging me to." One finger slid past the tight ring of muscle as my body clenched around him. Full and crazed, not wanting this to end. "Do you want that? Do you want to be a good girl and let me fuck your ass, Wildfire?"

"Oh God, please!"

He roared, slamming home, pumping his hips. The sounds of his skin smacking into my ass filling the air alongside the deliciously filthy sounds we both made. Louder and harder, until he thrust in one last time, and yelled his release. Sweat dripped onto my back as I collapsed onto the bed. Spent.

The weight of his body almost too much and not enough. After a few moments he stood, and I heard him shuffling around the room. A warm, wet cloth soothed my ravaged and satiated pussy as the wicked trio screamed in triumph.

He planted a soft kiss, untied the scarf over my eyes, and then went to toss the cloth into the hamper next to my bathroom door.

Naked and gorgeous, his body was bathed in moonlight for a second, and I caught sight of a tattoo on the side of his waist, just above his right hip. He went into the bathroom, and I heard the sound of running water before the light shut off. My eyes closed before I could say a word, and I fell fast asleep.

Dreaming of my cinnastalker, a touchdown run in by a sexy, masked tight end, and someone trying to steal my mango pico with a sly grin lighting up his green eyes.

Only to wake up a few hours later, alone.

With only a note, and my deliciously sore body, to know he had been here.

*You are mine now. And soon enough, I'll be yours. Sleep well, Wildfire. And I'll see you soon.*

# CHAPTER 15

## TY

"Wait, you're seeing someone? Behind my back?"

If I wasn't trying to figure out how the hell to tell Jessa who her masked man really was, I'd be giving Sebastian my best bromance, flirt with my eyes over Pom Guac ever. Because, fuck, dude was finally giving as good I he got.

I was so proud, and laid my hand over my heart. "Look at how far you've come, QB."

He snorted and motioned for another round. Nicky waved her fingers over her head with a smile. A boisterous din filled the Prickly Pear after this weekend's win, and even though we were regulars, there were more than a few unfamiliar faces in the crowd tonight. "For real, Simmons, it's not like either one of us is out of the other's sight this last month. When the hell did you meet a girl? And how are you hooking up without me knowing or you spilling all your secrets?"

"Miss my pillow talk?" Sebastian just glared at me, and I sighed. Long and hard, then dropped my head to the table. "She kinda doesn't know it's…me."

The beer he was drinking paused mid air. He blinked once, twice, then three times. "She doesn't...know it's you?"

I groaned, nodding into the table top.

"But, wait, I thought you said you hooked up with her?"

"More than hooked up. I'm gone, QB."

I half expected him to give me shit, or at least pretend to be jealous and tease me. Paybacks and all. But, nothing. I lifted my head a fraction of an inch and took a peek.

Phone in hand, Sebastian typed away, then glared at me. "Mads. Dude, how did you 'hook up' if this girl doesn't know who you are?"

"On the house," Nicky announced as she set down two and a tray filled with Pom Guac, chips, and tacos. "And Frankie said if you even try to pay, he's going to be very upset. So, don't make me deal with a crabby big brother, and enjoy, boys."

The sassy sister of the owner of the Prickly Pear patted Sebastian on the back and left with a wink. I let out a sigh. "I'm going to miss her. Good thing Love Beach isn't that far away."

"Stop trying to change the subject. How the hell did you hook up with a girl, and she doesn't know who the fuck you are?"

"Mask," I mumbled.

Sebastian went still, then laughed. "I thought you said mask," he chuckled.

Head down, I nodded.

"Shut the fuck up."

I lifted my head. "Yep." He just looked at me, not saying a word. I grabbed a taco, unwrapped it, and showed it in my mouth. But even the best damn taco in the world didn't compare to Jessa. Fuck. Now I just wanted to spend the fucking night eating tacos with her. Then licking her lips, tasting her. Watching her eyes close in ecstasy, either from the tacos or my mouth on her.

"A mask? Like you met while wearing a mask at some weird ass sex party?"

"What? No! Fuck no. I mean, I'm sure it happens. Somewhere. No. I know her."

"But she doesn't know you?"

I nodded, then shook my head. "Well, actually, she does. But she doesn't." I told him about how I saw her without telling him that the her in question was Jessa. His girlfriend's best friend. How I fell at first fucking sight and needed to know everything about her. How we started messaging. Flirting. How I watched her, the low key version, and that we sent DM's back and forth. Talking for hours at night.

Then hooking up. But she didn't know it was me, even afterwards.

Though I wanted to tell her. So fucking badly.

He grinned. "You kinky motherfucker. And here I thought you were Mr. Nice Guy."

"I am," I protested. "It's not like I creepy stalked her. But, Seb, I think I fucking love this girl."

With a smirk he shrugged, and said, "So tell her."

"It's not that easy."

"It is. If you know her, and she trusted you to tell you what she wanted, then a part of her knows it's you."

He said it like it was all so simple. But then again, I said the same things to him when he was afraid to be with Maddie. "Even if I snuck into her house and maybe lowkey stalked her with the security cameras in Magpie?"

He barked out a laugh. "You wouldn't be the first, my brother. How do you think Owen keeps an eye on Reid?" After he downed the rest of the amber liquid in his bottle, he pointed it back and forth between us. "Obsession is just another-" His eyes widened. "Wait. Magpie?"

*Shit.*

I stood, the chair scarping loudly as I scrambled to make a dash for the fucking bathrooms. "Be right back, don't leave without me." Winked, then tried to escape before the look of realization dawned over his handsome QB features.

Sebastian blocked me before I even took a step. Fuck. "Holy shit. The only girl who works at Magpie who isn't taken is-"

"Hey, Jessa, Maddie!" I said loudly, a bit obnoxiously, and with an extra large side of please don't say one more fucking word thrown at Sebastian.

Eyes wide, he glanced back and forth between the three of us before lopping his fingers in Maddie's belt, and giving her a very public display of affection as Jessa rolled her eyes behind them.

The action woke up my cock, and fuck if my hand didn't flex, wanting to relive making her ass red. My brat in all her bratty glory. *Shit, I really had to figure this out. And the sooner the better.*

"I'd say get a room, but today, I am all for PDA, with a side of Pom Guac. Ooh! And mango pico!" She took over Sebastian's seat, and helped herself. Her moans, the way she licked her lips after every fucking bite had me shifting so that my erection was at least partially hidden by the table.

I leaned forward, trying to avoid looking at Sebastian as he smirked.

"Holy. Fuck."

I froze, as Jessa, mouth wide open, stared at the spot my shirt rode up just enough so the side of my torso was visible.

Along with my tattoo.

Her eyes flew up to my face, then back to the tattoo. "You…it's…oh my fucking God."

"Jessa-" I reached for her hand, but she backed away, eyes narrowed. Fire practically leaping from her as she hissed,

"You're…I can't believe it didn't see it. I',m such a fucking fool." She spun and ran for the hall leading to the bathrooms, and I backed from the table.

Sebastian just smirked, arm around Maddie, who disentangled followed her best friend after planting a quick kiss on his cheek. "I told you I thought it was Ty."

He rolled his eyes and swatted her on the ass as she skirted out of his reach towards where Jessa ran off to, grinning.

My eyes darted back and forth. "What the fuck did she mean?"

"We all had a bet on how long before the two of you hooked up. I said secret hook up, Maddie said it was after you let her take you Pom Guac a few months ago."

My jaw went slack. "No shit?"

"The two of you were the only ones who didn't see the 'sexual tension', as Maddie liked to remind me. She was worried it would take away from our *bromance*, but I told her you liked to have things to focus on. Keeps all that pent up energy contained for the field." He glanced at the hall. "Go get your girl."

I didn't need to hear him say it twice. I weaved through the crowd, smiling at the congrats and pats on the back before stopping just outside the door of the ladies room.

"Jessa, he really likes you. We all saw it."

"But he lied, Mads."

"Did he? You can't tell me you didn't know it was him. I know you. You would never open up to someone unless you trusted them. Your heart knew it was Ty all along. Your head just took a little longer to catch up. It's like your last book."

"My last? Wait, you know?"

Maddie chuckled. "Reid and I have known since book two. The kink test? Dead giveaway. Plus we have bets on what kink is in your next book, Delena Bennett."

I pressed my ear against the door.

"That obvious?" Jessa asked.

"So obvious. Plus, you're an experimental brat. Ty's perfect for you. All cinnamon roll in the streets-"

"Cinnastalker in the sheets. And so good in the sheets," she said, voice all shady and filled with all the things we'd done. And still had to do. Such a long fucking list. "What do I do?'

"What you want."

"That simple?"

"Yep."

# CHAPTER 16

## JESSA

The door to the bathroom burst open, and in one fail swoop, Ty swept me up into his arms, claiming my mouth. Punishing, gentle, and all the things I dreamed of all rolled into one. My hands traced along his back, nails digging into his skin, his groan of approval making me want more.

"Um, I'll give you two a little privacy." Maddie snuck out, but neither one of us really noticed.

But we broke apart before we went any further. His eyes searched mine, fierce and ready for a fight.

"I've never wanted anyone like I want you, Jessa. I fucking love your fire. The way you never back down until you're ready. Your laugh. Your voice. Your heart. The way you look when you come, just for me. How you pour all your heart and soul into what you write. The love stories. The fucking sex, on the page and in my arms. And I want more. I want to make everyone fucking one of your fantasies come true. Leave you love notes just so I can imagine your lips parting when you read them. Watch you close your eyes when you smell coffee, or devour a damn taco. I want to lick and taste every single inch of your skin. Tell you bad dad jokes, feed you Australian licorice naked in bed. I fucking love you, Jessa. I have since the first moment I saw you. But if you can't-"

"Shut up, cinnastalker and fuck me, please. Then I'll yell at you. But can we keep the mask?" His green eyes twinkled.

"Hell yes." Hand made quick work of the skirt I wore, finger looping and pulling my panties to the side. The sound of his zipper sliding down made me so wet, when he slid home a second later, I was so ready that my body already tingled with my impending release.

"I don't think I can go slow," he growled. And damn if seeing his face, and the reflection of us in the mirror behind us didn't make my inner walls clench as he drove himself home. Unable to answer him, I scratched my nails down his back as our bodies gave and took in a dance we both understood. Even if we somehow fooled ourselves that it was all just a research project, our hearts knew better.

"Fuck, I'm coming," I gasped, and Ty took my face in his hands, not allowing me to look away as we both exploded. Fucking firecrackers and earthquakes and every damn fantasy come to life.

Seconds or hours later, he pulled out, gently cleaned us both, then slid my panties off. "Mine," he murmured as he put them in his pocket. His forehead rested against mine as our breathing slowly returned to normal. "I love you, Jessa."

I swooned. "I love you, too, Ty. I think I knew it was you, every message, Every time you left me something. The candy. Coffee. The car that night. But no more, "she stopped, as if she wasn't sure what to say, then squared her shoulders. "Fuck that. I want all the masks, and texts, and ordering me around. And the spankings."

"Fuck yes."

"Are you two done? There's a line, and Nicky says you

owe her tickets to the play off game!" Maddie said from the other side of the door.

We both chuckled as we headed out, heads held high.

"I think you should punish me for walking away. Wearing the mask. But this time, come in through my window," I added, licking his neck before heading back out into foray.

When we arrived at the table, Reid and Maddie high fived, Owen and Sebastian bought a round, and Ty slid his hand in mine. But no one said a word.

"So," he said, "who won the bet?"

Everyone started talking at once, and I couldn't help the smile that spread across my face.

Because I found my Cinnastalker, and my two besties weren't the only ones getting spankings from now on.

My phone pinged and I pulled it out. There was a message from right before Ty found me in the bathroom.

> Ready for a little more research, Wildfire?
> Cause I'm all yours. Like our HEA?

Hell, yes.

~

Enjoy Ty and Jessa? Leave a review!

Please make sure to check out all the other books in the You'll Be Mine series!!

And, if you need more hot sports action, you'll love my upcoming book in my Seattle Revenge Hockey series. Puck Me Harder, a part of Power Play Off the Ice, coming June 2024!

Want more of Ty and Sebastian's Bromance? Turn the page for a sneak peek at Hard Count!

# HARD COUNT

## SEBASTIAN

"Shittiest game you've ever played, Lockwood. And quite honestly, main office isn't exactly singing your praises."

Coach never blew smoke but fuck, he was right. And after nine years in the game, my arm wasn't like it used to be. Playing for Cleveland the past four seasons had been like being invited to dinner at your high school principal's house. At first, everyone likes you, until they realize you might be the troublemaker causing all the problems at school.

"The fact of the matter is, I can't have a quarterback leading my team who no one wants to fucking follow," he eyed me. "Or one who sleeps with his players' wives or girlfriends."

Fuck. "Not my fault she never told me her name," I held up my hands, "and Silva's wife showed up at my place in nothing more than a trench coat in the pouring rain." I called her a damn cab, but Silva showed up, after the bitch texted him, and laid me out flat before I could explain. Didn't help matters she'd slid into my DMs, and like an idiot, I'd played along not realizing who she was at first. When I tried to break it off, trench coat gate.

*Of course the rest of my line didn't believe my side of the story, and if your line doesn't protect you, you can't score.*

*Which means you can't win. And that translates to this fucking meeting.*

He sighed, and sat back into his chair. "Lockwood, I'm going to lay it out. I know your agent dropped you, HR doesn't want to touch this fucking thing with a damn ten foot pole, and if you were playing at the top of your game, I would do my damnedest to fight for you. But, you're not."

Allan Brandt informed me via text that he and his agency would no longer be representing me or my interests after this weekend.

*Basically, you're fucked, Bas.*

"The head office is activating the morals clause in your contract, effective immediately. And putting you on waivers."

My head shot up. Explained why Taft, the team legal head for Cleveland, entered the room just after Coach called me in a few minutes before. And why the tension in the air was so thick, you could cut it with a knife.

"No shit."

Taft cleared his throat, but Coach waved him off.

"Give us the room," he said with a shooing motion. Taft looked put off, but no one argued with Coach if they knew better. As Taft made his reluctant exit, Coach set his glasses on the desk and let out a breath as he leaned back in his chair. He shot a look at the door as it shut with a thud. "Lawyers don't get the nuances of the game. Or how chemistry and luck play into things."

Fuck me. I hung my head, not wanting to meet his eyes. My attitude was shit, and I knew it. He knew. Hell, the team knew it.

Especially Ty, the one guy on the team who made an attempt to stop my shitty attitude.

He eyed me a few times during practice, shaking his head, no doubt at my wasted talent.

No one wanted to protect a guy who acted like a world class dick.

And then something changed.

The only guy who stayed on for extra practice time with me. Of course, no one on the team except him knew I stayed, besides two of the trainers who left the door unlocked to the practice field twice a week for me after hours.

The first time Ty walked in on me to grab his lucky water bottle, he looked dumbstruck that I was still there, running snaps and throwing balls. Covered in sweat after a three and half hour practice, and a two hour workout on top of an hour run on the treadmill.

Typical day for me, though I never let on that I put in the extra time.

The intense physicality of it all kept the demons at bay. Chased away the regrets I had. Didn't help my attitude, but at least by the time I got home, I was too exhausted to think, let alone dream. Or if I did, I didn't remember shit.

After that first time, Ty 'left' with the rest of the squad, but came back fifteen minutes later. Each time, we'd run a few plays, simple runs. Neither of us said a word. Just two guys running the ball. Ty caught what I threw his way, sometimes a little out of his way to test our chemistry as the days went on. A little play action, and then we hit a few moments without having to say a word.

Fucking chemistry on the practice field that didn't translate anywhere else. And then I'd get on my bike or in my truck and leave.

Too bad the rest of the guys thought I was an asshole.

I let them. I knew I had a shitty attitude along with the walls I built up.

I wasn't the prince in a fucking fairytale. People thought I was the villain. The fans here were diehard, but even they were tired of my attitude.

I went from being the most loved QB a few years ago, to the most hated.

"Lockwood, the simple fact is that most of the organization thinks your career is over. And the way you've been handling yourself this year hasn't helped your case. But, I know more about you than you think." He stood and walked over to the window that overlooked the parking lot.

Empty, save for a few cars, since most of the team had left for the day. Including Taft's fancy fucking Jag. And my Audi, because I didn't use my bike when it rained. Fucking weather should've clued me in that today was going to be a shit show.

"I know you do extra practice after everyone leaves two or three times a week, and think no one knows. Train like a mad man. You might not get along with the entire team right now, but I've heard about the hospital visits, Lockwood." Hands in his pockets, he turned to face me, eyes shrewd and seeing far fucking more than I was comfortable with. "And Ty had a lot to say when I pulled him in a few days ago."

*Fucking Ty.* I ground my teeth together, jaw clenched and fists tight. But I kept my mouth shut.

"When he came to my office the other day, I have to admit, I thought it was going to be about your attitude. You two have had a few moments on the field, but without the rest of your team backing you up, it means shit, Lockwood."

Nothing I hadn't told myself a million times before. But I couldn't bring myself to care. Even when the damn fans began to boo whenever I took the field. It just made the anger and indifference stronger beneath it all.

"Then Simmons actually pleaded your damn case, even though the rest of the line seemed to miss out on whatever he saw. I noticed the two of you connecting on a level on the field, and when he told me he had been staying a few nights a week to run plays? I knew my instincts weren't far off. Now, I don't know what the hell your issues are, but I also know I wouldn't be where I am if someone hadn't offered me a path to make up for the shit I did when I was young and stupid."

I bristled at the comment, but deep down, I recognized what he was saying. To a point. "Doesn't matter if I'm getting cut, does it?"

"Lockwood, between Ty's bromance, no matter how strained your relationship is, and my instincts, you're not dead in the water." He sighed. "But, you're not staying in Cleveland, even with one game left in the season. I've called in a few favors. I'm not sure it'll come to anything. But for now, you're on waivers. And Simmons talked his agent into repping you if anyone calls."

Shit. I knew who Ty's agent was because he visited him a few times on game day, and shot me a look that made the other guys in the locker room back away.

Kellan Horne. From Fortress.

Well, fuck me. Talk about full circle.

I was so screwed.

~

Need more? Read all about #talldarkandasshole Sebastian Lockwood in Hard Count.

Don't miss out on Ty's story! And, curious how the golden retriever tight end for the Carolina Fury has a thing for the girl he watches in dark? Catch My Eye, coming March 26th.

# ACKNOWLEDGMENTS

Always my favorite part of the book going out into the wild process!

I have to admit, these last few months have been fast and furious. The ups and downs of author life can take a toll on the days when you feel like the rollercoaster is just trying to throw you for so many loops that you're not sure which way is up.

I am so grateful for the people I've sucked into my circle.

It's so true that the pages turned with the bridges burned bring you new and better things. A year ago, I almost gave up on my dream. It's not a time I ever want to relive, but, I know that if it wasn't for that time, I never would be where I am today.

It's brought people in my life, taken away the things that should never have been there, and given me so. Much more than I ever could have imagined.

Cassi Hart. I have an author crush on you. Big time. Thank you for inviting me into your world. And making me write my kind of stalker. You are an amazing person, and I simply adore you and all the other authors in the You'll Be Mine Series. What an amazing group to be included in.

To my team!! Street team and ARC team. For real, I appreciate each and every one of you. Not just for what you do for me, but for the love and passion you have for the romance community. Thank you for letting me be the hot, chaotic mess I am. And for reading and loving these people as much as I do.

To my GOOD GIRLS. Holy hell, y'all. There are not enough words, Vampire Diaries reels, or memes, hugs, or margs to show you how much you mean to me. Every time I want to break down in tears, stop, or just need to vent, you have me. You never let me stop. And I love you so freaking much.

To the ones I send silly DMs, dad jokes, and so much more. I appreciate you.

Jas, Gabs, Victoria, and Jess. Ty would not be who he is without you, and your belief that I could, indeed, pull this off. I love you all so damn much and cannot wait to hug you in person. Or go to Disney with you. Or both.

My boys. I hope someday, you look back and are proud of me. I hope that you chase your dreams because you see that I did it. I love you. SO VERY MUCH. And I know you are the reason my heart is so full. Please never read mommy's books. Or let me black out all the other stuff. I love you.

And to my one and only. I know I'm a mess and I don't always make sense. But, thank you for letting me be that mess. For all the crazy, the moods…and Saturday dinners.

## ALSO BY ARIANA ST. CLAIRE

### REVVED UP

When We Were Prequel (newsletter exclusive)

Track Me Down Duet Part One

Turn Me Loose Duet Part Two

Mistletoe Madness

Be My Secret Santa (A Stranger Session Christmas/Res & Piper prequel)

Claim My Heart (A Revved Up Standalone) *Coming 2024*

### STRANGER SESSIONS

When We Were Prequel

Trust Fall

Free Fall

Under the Mistletoe (Owen & Reid's First Christmas)

### DAD'S BEST FRIEND/REVVED UP STANDALONE

Steal My Kiss

A Little Naughty Christmas Gift (A Christmas Bonus Scene)

### SEATTLE REVENGE

Spicy Puck (F*** on the Ice Rink)

Puck, Love, and Mistletoe

Puck Me Harder (Power Play Off the Ice) 6/2024

Go Puck Yourself (Power Play Off the Ice: Snowed In) 11/2024

## OVERTIME

Hard Count

Touch Me Down

Catch My Eye (You'll Be Mine) 3/26/2024

## ALOHA HAWAII RELIEF SERIES/REVVED UP

Lei Me Down

Surf My Heart

## LOVE BEACH

Not So Blind Date with a Country Star (short story)

Summer with a Country Singer 6/13/2024

Merry With A Fake Boyfriend 11/2024

Spring Break with a Coach

## FROM VALENTINE'S TO VEGAS

Call My Bluff (Jett & Seguin)

## COLLECTED EDITIONS

Kiss Me, There's Mistletoe (Naughty & Nice Collected Edition)

## NAUGHTY CHRISTMAS IN JULY (MULTI-AUTHOR COLLECTION COMING JULY 2024!)

Deck My Halls

## BLIND DATE WITH A BOOK BOYFRIEND (MULTI-AUTHOR SERIES COMING SUMMER 2024)

July 2024

Well Played: A Charity Contemporary Romance Anthology (Oct. 16, 2024)

# ABOUT THE AUTHOR

Ariana can be found getting her Zen on while practicing hot yoga, going for a run, reading her favorite authors in the middle of the night, or having a bourbon on a Saturday while plotting the lives of her characters as they whisper and sometimes yell in her ear.

She lives her own Happily Ever After with her amazing husband, who shares her love of racing, comic books, and Firefly, along with her two spirited also amazing boys who love reading books under a blanket just as much as she does.

Subscribe to her newsletter here for all the news, updates, and exclusives!